Reid Wasn't About To Give Up Now. Or Ever.

He caught up with her as she walked quickly to the airport boarding gate. "Rachel, listen to me, please....

"I want to be around to see this child grown. I don't want to be a check in the mail and a weekend 'Uncle Daddy.'"

"What are you saying, Reid? You want to *live* with me and the baby?" She shook her head. "You can't imagine I'd be *kept*, like some high-class mistress."

"I don't want you to be my mistress, Rachel. What I'm saying is that I don't want to have to make an appointment to see my child. I want to be there. All the time. And there's only one acceptable way to do that."

"And that is?"

His answer made her mouth fall open. "What I want, Rachel, is for you to be my wife...."

Dear Reader,

It's not every month a *New York Times* bestselling writer joins the Desire family, so it's with great excitement that I get to announce that REBECCA BRANDEWYNE has become a part of Silhouette Books. Rebecca's *Wildcat* is not only a very special MAN OF THE MONTH, it's also her first full-length *contemporary* romance. You'll fall in love with rough and rugged oilman Morgan McCain as he spars with spirited Cat Devlin; and you'll never forget their passionate love story!

I'm equally thrilled about the rest of October's lineup. Award winner Cindy Gerard makes her Silhouette Desire debut with the sensuous Western *The Cowboy Takes A Lady*. And if you're a fan of BJ James, don't miss *A Wolf In The Desert*, book #3 in her MEN OF THE BLACK WATCH series.

And if you enjoy time travel—or even if you don't—you'll *love* Cathie Linz's *A Wife in Time*. Cathie's delightful dialogue and sexy stories are, well, *timeless*. Talented author Audra Adams brings us a dramatic story of powerful love and possible betrayal with *The Bachelor's Bride*.

Bringing you a *brand-new*, never-before-published writer is always a special moment for an editor, and I'm *very* enthusiastic about our PREMIERE author Christine Pacheco. Don't miss her first published book, *The Rogue and the Rich Girl*.

Silhouette Desire: we've got something for everyone!
So enjoy...

Lucia Macro
Senior Editor

Please address questions and book requests to:
Silhouette Reader Service
U.S.: 3010 Walden Ave., P.O. Box 1325, Buffalo, NY 14269
Canadian: P.O. Box 609, Fort Erie, Ont. L2A 5X3

AUDRA ADAMS

THE BACHELOR'S BRIDE

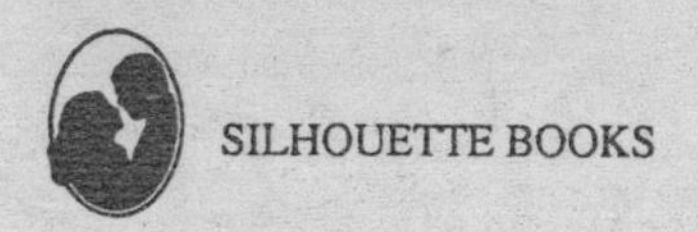

ISBN 0-373-05959-0

THE BACHELOR'S BRIDE

This edition published by arrangement with Harlequin Books S.A.

Printed in U.S.A.

Books by Audra Adams

Silhouette Desire

Blue Chip Bride #532
People Will Talk #592
Home Sweet Home #695
Devil or Angel #783
Rich Girl, Bad Boy #839
His Brother's Wife #912
The Bachelor's Bride #959

AUDRA ADAMS

loves to dream up her characters' stories while lying on the beach on hot summer days. Luckily, her Jersey-shore home offers her the opportunity to indulge in her fantasies.

She believes that falling in love is one of the most memorable experiences in a person's life. Young or old, male or female, we can all relate to those exquisitely warm feelings. She knows that stories of romance enable us to tap into that hidden pleasure and relive it through characters.

An incurable romantic, Audra is in love with love, and hopes to share that optimism with each and every one of her readers.

Special thanks to two special men…
Jim Reid, for lending his name and his inspiration…
-and-
Frank Banas, for teaching me the difference between
"separate" and "spread."

Prologue

Everything was white. The walls were white, the curtains billowing out from the dark, open windows were white, the bed was very white, its sheets, its satin comforter, the netting hanging from the ceiling. All pristine, blemishless.

White.

She cradled her head in her arm as she laid back against the smooth pillow. A brilliant moon bathed the room in pale light. Her eyes were wide open and she watched him approach her, slowly, steadily, a cigarette in his hand. He, too, was dressed in white, a casual summer suit and half-buttoned shirt.

He smiled, and she smiled back at him. She didn't move as he sat on the edge of the bed. His eyes roamed her face, her body, caressing her. They were green, like emeralds with a fire ring of blue around the outer rims. She said something and he laughed, the corners of his eyes crinkling, making him look far less forbidding than before.

He put out the cigarette in the white ashtray, leaned forward and kissed her. She let him. He felt wonderful. His lips were cool as they brushed against hers. He pulled back and stared at her, the smile gone, and in its place was another look, not the forbidden one, but something different.

Desire.

She'd seen it before in a man's eyes, of course, but never like this. This was intense, and a blip of fear invaded her belly. Or was it excitement? She raised her hand to his face to brush away a strand of very blond hair, and he turned into her palm. His skin was warm, dry, smooth.

He moved closer, his face only inches away from hers. "I want to make love with you," he whispered.

"Yes . . ." she answered with a long hissing sound that he cut off as his mouth descended once again.

He parted her lips with his tongue this time and swept inside her mouth with the power and finesse of a tempest at sea. She had never been kissed like this, had never felt a mouth this hot, this wet, this controlling. She could only follow his lead, do his bidding, and she did, willingly.

His hands touched her, moving up her arms ever so slowly to her collarbone and onto the tops of her breasts. He played there for a moment until the straps of her sundress fell from her shoulders. With a slight tug, he had it to her waist, baring her breasts to his burning gaze.

He flicked his fingers against her nipples, the peaks so sensitive, they hardened immediately under his ministrations. He smiled again, murmuring words of praise that twisted her insides with their meaning.

She closed her eyes as his mouth replaced his fingers, and once again she was taken by surprise by the heat of him. Her body arched. He ran his hands down her sides, lifted her dress and caressed the insides of her thighs with featherless movements of his fingertips.

"Open," he said, his head pillowed on her breast, his breath fanning her sensitive skin.

Obediently she spread her legs, anxious for him to touch her. But he took his time, teasing her as he ran a fingertip into the elastic band of her panties, back and forth, pulling the material, stretching it until he managed to get past the barrier to the sweetness that lay beyond.

She called out when he touched her, and he raised his head to kiss her once again, taking her mouth whole, swallowing her moan as his fingers grew bolder. He dipped into her, stroked her. She felt her body melt against his fingers. She was wet, hot, needy.

And she wanted more. Her hands roamed inside his open shirt. She splayed her fingers across the expanse of his chest, running her fingernails through the soft tufts of hair, scratching her way down his body until she reached his waistband.

His fingers hesitated for the briefest moment before he continued the slow, steady, intimate stroking. He sat back and watched as her fumbling fingers unbuckled his belt, freed the fastening, and unzipped his pants. His eyes were intense as she ran her fingers over the length of him. He was smooth, hot and hard, a reward, she felt, for her persistence.

They stared into each other's eyes as their hands, their fingers, continued to drive their bodies to the brink. She was the first to look away. She shut her eyes tightly as her body took control, pulsing to the rhythm of his stroking, building, climbing toward a light so blinding she felt she would fall into it.

"Now," he said, and she did not argue.

Within seconds his body covered hers, and he was there. *She had never been this full, this stretched, this consumed by a man. Her hips rose and fell in tandem with his movements. They danced the ancient dance of men and women in perfect harmony, so sweet, so pure, so wonderful that she could not stop the spasms of pleasure when they came. So she didn't try. She rose to greet them, rejoicing in the way he made her feel, rejoicing in her own ability to* feel *this at all, rejoicing in his response as he tensed and followed her headlong into the burst of light.*

After a long moment he raised himself up onto his elbows. His eyes were mesmerizing. They sparkled in the bright moonlight. Again he smiled, and the eyes crinkled. He kissed her nose, and she smiled, too.

She studied his face, so tanned and handsome with his high cheekbones, strong jaw and very blond hair falling down across his forehead. A nice face, a trustworthy face, a face she could love, she thought.

A face in a dream. . . .

One

The dot was blue. She held it up to the light to double check. Just in case she'd made a mistake.

For the second time.

No. There was no doubt. It was blue all right.

Rachel Morgan slowly sat on the commode in the bathroom of her tiny studio apartment. She exhaled a long-held, overly hopeful breath. There would be no point in taking the test a third time. The results were sure to be the same.

She was pregnant.

The question was, *how?*

Her hands began to shake as she lost her adrenalin high. This couldn't be happening, couldn't be real. Rachel hadn't had a serious relationship since she'd moved to New York City two years ago after her mother's death and the breakup of her engagement to Tom. There was *no one* in her life—if you could call the mess she'd made of things to date a life. Biting her lip, she fought back tears.

Jobless. And now pregnant.

But again, the how came back to haunt her. She was a rational human being. There was no such thing as an immaculate conception—at least not that she knew of, not in this day and age, and not to someone as imperfect as she. So there had to be another explanation. Her stomach churned.

Which meant that The Dream had to be real.

The phone rang and she forced herself to rise and walk into the L-shaped room that served as her kitchen, living room and bedroom. She sat on the edge of her Murphy bed and lifted the receiver.

"Hello?"

"Rachel? Trudy. I'm glad I caught you. I may have a lead on a job. One of our suppliers is looking—"

"I'm pregnant."

"What?"

"You heard me."

"How?"

"Darned if I know. I'm sitting here trying to figure it out." She didn't mention the nausea or the shaking.

"Don't move," Trudy said. "I'll be right over."

A half hour later Rachel's buzzer sounded. She pressed the button and leaned into it, then waited at the door until she heard the elevator ping. Opening the door, she rested against the jamb and watched her best friend in the entire world walk toward her.

A tall, slim, gorgeous redhead, Trudy Levin was a walking neurosis—ambitious, hyper, driven to succeed in the high-powered world of the cosmetics industry.

When Rachel had first arrived in the city two years ago, she had "hick" written all over her. They'd met on the subway when Rachel had gotten hopelessly lost going crosstown. Trudy, a rare Manhattan native, had rescued her, yapping on her heels like a mother hen. They'd been fast friends ever since.

"I don't believe this," Trudy said, brushing past Rachel as she hurried into the apartment. But then, Trudy didn't walk, she hurried—everywhere.

Rachel made a slow turn and shut the door behind her.

"Lock it," Trudy said, dropping her oversize bag onto a kitchen chair.

Rachel smiled and obeyed. Trudy was always ordering her around, mostly with warnings on how to survive in the big, bad city. Rachel knew she did it out of love, and found it no chore to deal with her friend's paranoia.

"Now, tell me what happened."

Rachel lifted the wand off the counter with more aplomb than she felt and held it out for Trudy's inspection. "Blue."

"I don't believe it," Trudy repeated.

"How do you think I feel?" Rachel said.

To cover her agitation, Rachel busied herself at the sink. She filled the teakettle with water, then placed it on the front burner. With a flick of her wrist, the flame erupted underneath.

"I'm hurt. Didn't I tell you all about Jake when I met him? Didn't I fill you in on every dirty detail of every date? Why didn't you tell me you were seeing someone?" Trudy asked, a puzzled, pained expression on her face.

"Because I'm not."

"Then who..."

Rachel shook her head. "I don't know."

"That's impossible."

"No, it's true. I have no idea who the father is."

Trudy walked over to Rachel. She gripped Rachel's shoulders in her hands and turned her around so that they faced each other.

"Look at me." Rachel complied, and Trudy's voice softened when she noticed the tears threatening. "Honey, I know you're a country girl and all that, but even you know that this isn't something you pick up from a toilet seat at a department store."

Rachel attempted a smile. "I know..."

"Then who—"

The teakettle began to whistle and Rachel lifted it off the burner and extinguished the flame. She held the steaming pot aloft as she looked up at Trudy. "It must have been the dream."

"Dream?"

"You remember, the one I told you about. The one I had when I was sick with the flu."

"The White Dream?"

Rachel gave her a wry grin. "Yes. The White Dream."

Trudy dropped into the chair. "Okay. Let's figure this out."

"Would you like a cup of tea?" Rachel asked.

"Yeah. Lemon and a half—"

"I know. A half packet of sweetener."

Rachel set the small, two-seater table with napkins and spoons and prepared the mugs of tea. She looked up at Trudy, feeling herself steady a bit now that her friend was here, now that she had someone to share this with.

Once they were seated opposite each other and the first sip had been taken, Trudy leaned forward and patted her hand. "Now, tell me from the beginning."

"I don't remember the beginning. Just the end."

"Then tell me the end."

Rachel took a second small sip of the hot liquid. "It must have happened the night I got sick. Remember that?"

"Yeah," Trudy said. "You came with me to the launch party for the new perfume. You had a bad cold."

"And I was on antibiotics. I shouldn't have gone out, but you insisted."

"So it's my fault."

Rachel shook her head. "No, of course not. I just remember you insisting that I go. You wanted me to get out, meet people, maybe make a contact for a job."

"Right. We stayed at the party until late. We were almost the last to leave. I remember it was so crowded at the armory I couldn't find you. I walked the hall a hundred times, but you were nowhere to be found. It was like you disappeared."

"I don't remember any of that."

"I found you out front, sitting on a stoop, with your head against the railing. You'd fallen asleep. When I woke you up, you were white as a ghost and felt sick to your stomach. We left right then. I hailed a cab and brought you up here and put you to bed. Do you remember any of this?"

"No. I just remember going with you to the party. I remember walking into the hall, having something to drink...some kind of punch—"

"The punch was spiked."

Rachel stared into space. "I don't know about that, either. The rest of the night is a blank."

Trudy took her hand. Rachel noticed the concern in her face.

"Tell me about the dream," Trudy said.

"It's hard. It's so jumbled."

"Try."

She took a breath and let it out slowly. "There was a man, and we...we were..."

"Having sex."

"Yes." Rachel blushed.

"In the white room?"

"Yes."

"And when did you first have this dream?" Trudy asked.

"The first time was when I had the flu. I was sick for two weeks, and I just kept having the dream over and over again. Then it stopped."

"And that was how long ago?"

"Six weeks."

"How late are you?" Trudy asked.

"Six weeks."

"Mystery solved."

"Oh, Trudy. It can't be true!"

"Honey, you disappeared for at least an hour that I know of, probably more. You must have left with someone. Now all we have to do is figure out who." She tapped her finger to her lips. "Describe him to me. Maybe I can help."

"He was dressed in white."

"Great help," Trudy said. "It was mid-June. All the men there were dressed in white."

"He was tall. Blond." She paused. "And he had green eyes."

"Now we're getting somewhere."

Rachel shut her eyes, allowing the dream to swirl around inside her head, pulling it back from her memory. She felt a shiver inside. "He smoked. And had a great smile. His eyes crinkled—" she opened her eyes and pointed to the corners "—right here. He had a low voice, kind of Rod Stewart-ish." She looked at Trudy. "Well? Anything?"

"I don't know. Maybe. What else?"

"His mouth. He had the greatest mouth."

"In what way?" Trudy asked.

Rachel looked away. "I don't know how to describe it." She stared at her friend and felt the heat of embarrassment rise to her face.

Trudy ignored it. "This is no time to be shy, Rachel. Try."

"Hot."

"Hot?"

"Yes, his mouth was...hot."

Trudy tilted her head and pursed her lips. "You seem to be remembering more than you thought."

Rachel studied her hands. "I guess I am."

"Anything else?"

"Not that I can think of." She bit her lip. "Wait, there is one more thing. He had a slight accent. Very slight. I couldn't tell exactly what. English. Maybe French—"

"French Canadian."

"What? You know who he is?" Rachel asked, excited.

"I'm not sure. But he sounds like someone I may know."

"Who? For heaven's sake, Trudy, tell me, who?"

"My boss."

"Not Reid James!"

"Yes, Reid James. The nineties answer to Robert Redford."

Rachel put her hand to her mouth. "Oh, my God. I thought it was a dream."

Trudy looked down in the vicinity of Rachel's stomach. "Apparently not."

Reid wanted the meeting to be over. Now. He was beyond bored, teetering awfully close to comatose. Why did these people go on so? Why didn't they just say what they had to say and leave?

He put a hand up to his chin and nodded in their direction, pretending to be listening, hoping that his response was appropriate. Of course, it wasn't just these people who bored the hell out of him. It was everyone and everything in his life.

At thirty-five he'd seen it all and done it all . . . and then some. He had put together a multimillion dollar conglomerate of varied and sundry corporations in a ten-year frenzy of activity that earned him equal amounts of praise and criticism.

But now he was tired. And he was done. Let someone else—or a dozen someone elses—run the businesses. He wanted out. He'd been thinking about it for a long time now, ever since his mother had died three years ago. He'd proven all he'd had to prove to her, and to his father, too, who'd finally acknowledged his existence only after he'd made his first million.

But getting out, letting go, was easier said than done. The time never seemed right. There was always another meeting to attend, another crisis to face, another "fire" to put out.

Not anymore. His interest was nil. He was done, through. Finis.

He needed only one thing to let go completely—and that, he feared, was not so easy to find.

He needed another reason to go on living.

"Excuse me," Reid said as he stood. His words stopped the speaker in midsentence, and out of deference to him, the room was silent. "I have to leave," he said, and did.

He felt their eyes on his back as he made his way to the door, but of course, no one said a word. No one ever did anymore.

No one questioned him. No one challenged him.

He was omnipotent.

He strolled back to his office, in no real hurry to get there, stopping along the way to talk to employees who greeted him. He knew their names, each and every one of them from the mail boy on up. A name was something that was important to him. He'd had to fight for what should have been his from birth, and when he finally had the right to use it, he gave it up, opting instead for a play on the name he'd been given by the nuns in the orphanage.

His back straightened as he walked, recalling all too well the perfect posture drilled into him by the saintly but tough-as-nails Ursuline Sisters.

Charlotte Mercier, his executive assistant, sat at her desk in his inner sanctum. She effectively ran the office now, answering his mail, signing his name to letters. He trusted her implicitly and would have no qualms about handing the reins over to her if he ever left. Whenever he mentioned the possibility, she pretended to be shocked by the thought of it, but he had no doubt that she could handle the responsibility.

She glanced up at his approach and handed him a stack of pink slips with phone calls to be returned. He leafed through them, quickly dropping the majority back on her desk for her to handle or dispose of. This exercise was just a formality. He returned very few calls anymore. Charlotte expertly picked through them, putting aside those she would return, and trashing those she would not.

One did catch his eye. "When did Mazelli call?" he asked.

"About a half hour ago."

He nodded. Eddy Mazelli was someone who did interest him. Eddy was a private investigator who'd been recommended to him as the best in the business. Problem was that in the six weeks since he'd signed on, the man had come up empty.

Not that he'd had much to go on.

Frustration gnawed at Reid like a cancer. He hated not being in control, but this was one situation where that had never been the case. Not from the first.

He wished he could get that night out of his head, but he couldn't. Maybe it was because it had been such a long time since he'd been with anyone like her. Scratch that. He'd *never* been with or even *known* anyone like her. The time they'd spent together had been surreal. She'd been so relaxed, uninhibited, funny, soft, feminine, lovely, hot, sexy, and...something else...loving. Things he'd never had nor expected from a woman.

It had scared the holy hell out of him.

They'd made love, and it wasn't so much that they'd done anything different or out of the ordinary. No, it wasn't the *way* they'd made love, but what had happened between them *as* they'd made love.

Reid had lost himself in her. He'd heard about such things happening, of course, but it had never happened to him, not in all the years with any of the women he'd bedded. *Never.*

So the fear came first, but it was quickly followed by exhilaration, and later, much later, by this frustration that had gripped him since and not let go.

She'd disappeared. He'd left her for only a few moments to get a drink, and when he'd returned she was gone. Poof! Up in smoke. As if she'd been a dream.

But she was no dream. Her scent had clung to his pillow for days afterward and, silly man that he was, he'd fought with his housekeeper not to change the sheets, acquiescing only when the woman threatened to quit.

No. It had been all too real, and it—she—had consumed his thoughts, his nights, his days ever since.

"Get Mazelli on the phone for me," he said to Charlotte, and walked toward his office.

"Trudy Levin is in there waiting for you," Charlotte said as she lifted the receiver.

"What does she want?" Reid asked, hand on the doorknob.

Charlotte shrugged. "She wouldn't say. Only that she had to see you. Important."

He nodded. "Okay. I'll see her. Get Mazelli." He opened the door.

"Oh, and she has a woman with her."

Charlotte's voice followed Reid as he entered his office. The room was large, taking up the better quadrant of the top floor of the office building that he owned. It was bright, with all the draperies pulled back to allow the maximum amount of sunlight inside. He'd picked the room purposely for that, one of his greatest weaknesses being the sun on his face.

Trudy stood and turned to him as he entered. She smiled. "Hi, Reid."

He smiled, too. He liked her. She was one of his best employees. Smart. Loyal. Ambitious. All the things he liked to think he was.

He took a step closer to his desk. "Trudy. What can I do for you?"

And then his eye caught sight of a dark-haired woman standing by the corner window. Her hand was entwined with the material of the drapery as she admired the view. At that moment she turned and looked at him over her shoulder. Reid squinted against the light that framed her face like a halo.

Recognition came like a fist to his solar plexus.

"Rachel." It was a harsh whisper.

Trudy sighed, just loud enough to divert his attention for an instant. "I see," she said, "there's no need for an introduction."

Two

"You know my name?"

Reid took a step closer. "Only that it's Rachel. Nothing more."

She looked the same to him, the only difference being her mood. The first time she'd been smiling, carefree, loose. Now she was nervous, uptight, strung out. But the eyes were the same, a soft gray rimmed in a black so dark it matched the color of her hair.

The buzzer sounded and Charlotte's voice filtered through the intercom. "Mazelli on line one."

As if to insure that she wouldn't disappear again, Reid kept his eyes riveted on Rachel as he walked to his desk and lifted the receiver.

He pointed to her. "Don't move," he said, then pressed the button for line one. "Yes." He tapped his fingers on the leather blotter on his desk and listened for a short time. "Fine. Send me a bill." He looked up at Rachel, and their eyes locked. "Yes. That's right. I no longer need your services."

Reid cradled the receiver. He remained stone-still, staring at Rachel as if she were a phantom. Rachel stared back. Trudy coughed. "Maybe I *should* introduce you," she said. "Rachel Morgan, Reid James."

"Hello," Rachel said softly.

"Hello? That's all you have to say to me? After what you've done?"

Rachel looked to Trudy then back to Reid. "I—I don't understand. What have I done?"

Reid stood for a moment, mouth agape. He realized what he must look like and purposely shut it.

"This is a joke, right?"

Rachel shook her head slowly. "No."

Turning to Trudy, Reid said, "Would you mind leaving us alone for a little while?"

Trudy hesitated. "I don't know if I should. She's not used to your rages, Reid. You look like you're ready to kill someone."

"Go along, Trudy, and don't worry. I gave up killing women years ago."

Trudy shook her head and gave him a patronizing grin. "Maybe I should stay."

"No. There are things I need to say that are private."

"I think I know what they are," Trudy said.

"Do you?" Reid said with an arch of his brows. "That's interesting, because I don't."

His fury was simmering, evidently close to the surface. Trudy glanced at Rachel. She was shaking.

"It's all right," Rachel said to her friend, her voice trembling. "Go. Please."

Trudy walked to the door. "All right. But I'm waiting right outside. Scream if you need me." She paused with her hand on the doorknob and turned to look at Reid. "That goes for either one of you."

When she was gone, Reid stepped from around his desk. He walked over to the sitting area and placed his hand on the back of a Queen Anne chair.

"Sit," he said softly, and when she didn't move right away, added, "Please."

It was not a word he used often, if at all, and it didn't roll off of his tongue easily, but he didn't want to scare her away. Not again. *If* that's what he had done the first time. He didn't know, and that was the problem. He had to know who she was and what had happened. Never one to look a gift horse in the mouth, he wasn't about to blow this opportunity, this tremendous stroke of good luck, and lose her again.

"Please," he repeated, and this time she complied, moving toward him, then around him before sitting in the chair.

He sat on the couch across from her with only the width of the coffee table separating them.

Rachel placed her hands on her knees, palms down. "Can you tell me what happened that night?" she asked.

Reid arched his brows. "I was going to ask you that question."

Rachel shook her head. "I don't know. I thought it was all a dream up until now."

"A dream?"

"Yes... You see, I became quite ill after. The flu or some such virus. Whatever the case, I was in pretty bad shape. I passed out the night of the party, and I'm afraid I don't remember very much about it. Trudy said you were the host."

"Yes... Our new perfume launch party at the armory. We met there," he said, choosing his words carefully. "We talked..."

"Yes?"

Was she for real? Did she actually think that he would believe she didn't remember any of this?

"We left together." Rachel's eyes widened. She leaned forward, urging him on with a nod of her head. "We walked for a while," he continued, "and ended up by my place. Do you remember any of this?"

"No," she said softly. "What happened then?"

"And then you came with me upstairs."

"To your apartment?"

"At first."

"And after?"

"To my bedroom."

Rachel's gaze dropped to her hands. She felt the heat rise to her face.

"Look at me," he said, and she lifted her eyes. "You really don't remember?"

"No. I was on antibiotics. I had something to drink. The punch, I think—"

"The punch was almost all vodka."

"That's what Trudy said. I don't know if the combination of the two had something to do with it, but I blacked out the rest of the evening."

"You seemed perfectly all right." He paused. "More than all right."

"But I wasn't."

"You don't remember making love—"

"No...yes...but only afterward. I thought it was a dream."

"You said that. What made you change your mind?"

Rachel blew out a breath to steady her nerves. She was trembling so badly she had to sit back in the chair and grip the armrests to stop herself from visibly shaking.

"Something's happened."

"What's happened?" he asked.

"I'm pregnant."

Reid stared at her. He didn't think anything could shock him more than her unexpected appearance. But she'd topped that. And then some. He kept his expression neutral, no easy feat when his heart was thumping so hard in his chest he thought the buttons on his shirt would pop.

"And you're here to claim that I'm the father?"

"There's no other explanation," she said.

"I could think of a few."

Rachel's hands formed into fists. She had to remain in control. This was difficult enough without her losing it. Of course he would be skeptical. Who wouldn't be? Yet he had a right to know, whether he believed her or not.

She licked her lips. "I know what you're thinking—"

"You haven't the faintest idea what I'm thinking," he said with a raw politeness that bordered on contempt.

"Yes, I do. You think I'm after money or something. Well, I'm not. I don't want anything from you." She stood. "When Trudy and I finally figured out what must have happened, I asked her to bring me here. I thought you had a right to know. No more, no less." Rachel eased herself away from the chair and headed for the door. "I won't bother you anymore."

"Stop right there," he said.

"I'm not one of your underlings, Mr. James, you can't order me around."

"Come back." When she didn't move, he gritted his teeth and added, "Please..."

Rachel looked across the room into crystal green eyes. The intensity of his gaze was overpowering and it propelled her forward. She stopped a few feet from him. "I have nothing else to say to you," she said.

"Well, I have some things I'd like to say to you, if you don't mind."

"Go ahead."

Reid moved away from the couch. His mind was reeling. With the ease and grace of a man used to getting his own way all the time, he walked over to his desk. He lifted a gold cigarette case off the mahogany top and flipped it open, extracting one and slipping it between his lips.

"Cigarette?" he asked, then added, "No. I forgot. You don't smoke. Tried it once when you were sixteen and made yourself sick."

Rachel's chin came up as a chill ran down her spine. She had told him things about herself. Details about her life. Yet all she had from him came through Trudy and what she'd read in the papers. All secondhand.

Except, that is, for the child she carried.

A wave of weakness overcame her and she swayed. "I'd like to sit down," she said in a small voice, and moved toward the leather chair in front of his desk.

"How about some coffee? Or tea?" he asked.

"Tea would be wonderful."

Reid pressed the intercom and placed the order with Charlotte.

"You don't look well," he said, concern in his voice.

"I'm fine. Just a little dizzy." She looked up at him. "Normal, I'm told, under the circumstances."

He gave her a curt nod and lit his cigarette. He took a long drag into his lungs as Charlotte brought in a cup of tea on a tray. She carried his finest china service, the one reserved for important guests, foreign dignitaries and the like. Reid caught his assistant's eye and questioned her with a glance. She smiled, a Mona Lisa smile that said she knew too much.

Damn Trudy. He'd better nip this bit of news in the bud or the entire building would know about it before five o'clock quitting time.

"Thank you," Rachel said as she accepted a cup from Charlotte.

"You're welcome, dear," Charlotte said. "If you need anything else, just call."

"That will be all, Charlotte," Reid said, dismissing her.

She smiled again as she left, and Reid gave her an imperceptible shake-of-the-head warning before returning his attention to the woman across from him.

As Rachel doctored the tea, Reid studied her through a haze of smoke, his eyes hooded, his brain racing. He attempted to conjure up that night once again, more pragmatically this time, without the warm, fuzzy feeling that always seemed to engulf him whenever he thought of her.

That day had been hell. By five o'clock he'd had a raging headache, and the last thing he'd wanted to do was to make the obligatory appearance at the perfume launch party. But he'd relented and agreed to attend. He'd milled around the room several times, shaking hands, making nice to all the media people. The place was packed to capacity, invitations having spawned invitations like rabbits in a warren. They'd rented the armory for the event, which was only blocks from his town house, and the temptation to cut out early was too great to ignore. He had been just about to do that when he'd spotted her.

Like a scene out of an old movie, the hoards of people had faded into the background as their eyes met across the room. Without much thought, he'd changed direction and walked over to her. She'd smiled, and the pounding in his head had seemed to subside. They'd talked party talk, and she'd made him laugh. No easy feat under the best of circumstances, but that night of all nights it had seemed almost miraculous.

He'd asked her to get some air, go for a walk, and she'd accepted. Moving slowly through the crowd, they'd managed to leave without anyone noticing. The night was warm, humid, and after a block or two their clothing had stuck to them. He hadn't planned it, but they'd ended up near his town house. He'd invited her up for a cool drink, and she'd accepted.

The memories swirled around him as he gazed across the desk at her sipping her tea. She glanced at him over the rim of the cup.

The warm fuzzies returned. He couldn't remember the rest of the evening without them. She'd been so...real.

They'd talked as if they'd known each other all their lives. When she'd commented on the decor, he'd taken her on a tour of the town house, ending up in his top-floor bedroom. She'd teased him about the size of his bed, and he'd jokingly told her to test it out. With lazy informality, she'd stretched out on his bed, luxuriating in the feel of his white satin sheets.

It was then that their eyes had met once again and the same tug that had pulled him to her at the party had brought him to sit on the edge of the bed.

She'd been so unselfconscious that it had seemed like the most natural thing in the world to lean forward and kiss her.

And then he'd lost it. All sense of time, place, reality...control. They'd made love with such freedom, such *comfort*, it had seemed as if they'd been at it for years.

Which was why he couldn't forget it.

And if it had been that special for him, it had to have been that way for her, as well.

Which was also why he wasn't buying her claim that she couldn't remember any of this.

Was it all an act? He couldn't know, not yet. Not until he'd had a chance to check her out. But she knew Trudy Levin and that was a plus in her favor. Trudy had been with him a long time, and he trusted her completely.

But he'd been this "baby" route before. He'd reached a plateau in life where he was fair game to all around him. When he was in his twenties, he'd been wrongfully slapped with a paternity suit, and while he was able to medically prove the woman wrong and win the case, it had been an expensive and embarrassing undertaking.

Since then he'd become twice shy when it came to relationships. In the last several years, despite newspaper items to the contrary, there had been fewer and fewer women in his life, to the point where he spent a good part of the year alone. And when he chose otherwise, he was particularly cautious, almost to the point of paranoia when it came to using protection. And such had been the case with Rachel.

But condoms didn't always work—his parents could attest to that—and for that he owed her the benefit of the doubt.

"Better?" he asked as she placed the teacup on the tray.

"Yes. Much." She looked up at him. "What did you want to ask me?"

"If what you say is true—"

"It is."

"Then, I suppose I'm asking what you intend to do."

Rachel toyed with the delicate handle of the teacup. "There are options . . . choices," she said softly.

"Yes. Have you made any decision yet?"

She shook her head slowly. "No." She looked up at him. "I haven't."

They stared at each other for the longest time, all those troubling questions with no satisfactory answers hanging in the air between them.

Reid squashed the cigarette in an ashtray. "I'd like to be included in that decision-making process, if I may?"

"Then you believe me?"

He sat back in his chair. "Not necessarily."

"Then why bother? When I walk out of here today, you don't ever have to see me again. I promise not to involve you in any way."

"There is always the possibility that you are telling the truth," he said. "If that's the case, Rachel, have no doubts, I will be involved. I take my responsibilities seriously."

"I'm not your responsibility. I can take care of myself."

"We'll see about that," he said.

"Are you going to investigate my background, Mr. James?" she asked sarcastically.

He stood. "As a matter of fact, I am, Rachel. And, oh, let's dispense with the formalities. A little late for that, don't you think? Call me Reid." He paused and pinned her with his eyes. "You did that night... over and over again."

Rachel's throat went dry. She swallowed. "I don't remember."

Reid came to her, and she looked up at him. His face was intense, his eyes as green as a meadow in spring. Placing one hand on each armrest, he effectively trapped her in the chair.

"Then let me refresh your memory."

His mouth came down on hers. Rachel remained absolutely still with no thought of resistance. Her eyes fluttered closed as his lips touched hers. As if it were the most natural thing in the world, she parted her lips for him. And as night follows day, his tongue swept into her mouth, met hers, mated, and danced a lovers' dance.

The first thing that registered in Rachel's mind was the heat. She remembered that with crystal clarity. Then his scent washed over her, his taste, and a flash flood of memories engulfed her. A powerful twinge of desire unfurled in her belly as his heat drifted down through her mouth into all the vital parts of her body.

Her pulse accelerated to an alarming rate. Her head lolled back against the chair and he followed, opening his mouth wider, deepening the kiss, taking as much as she was willing to give. More.

Reid felt like an alcoholic denied drink for too long, freed at last to have a taste, just this one and no more. His heart and head pounded in tandem as he drank his fill. She whimpered, and the sound vibrated into him, his mouth, his heart, his soul.

His arms began to tremble from exertion and something else he didn't dare name, and the fear returned.

He released her.

They stared at each other, their faces only inches apart, their breathing labored as if they'd been running.

"I'm sorry," he said softly, uncharacteristically apologizing, not knowing why, only feeling the need to do so.

Rachel touched her swollen lips with her fingertips. "Why did you do that?" she asked.

His hands in fists, Reid took a step back from her and shook his head as if to clear it, more for himself than to answer her question.

He half turned and looked at her. "I had to see if your dream had just been my imagination."

Rachel nodded, knowing what he meant, understanding that he needed verification that they had, indeed, been together, been more to each other than casual acquaintances at a party. The baby notwithstanding—it still didn't seem quite real enough to her yet—like he, she'd needed some proof now, some tangible evidence that the dream had, indeed, been real.

And if nothing else, the kiss had proved that.

To both of them.

He'd kissed her, but she'd known how to kiss him back. She'd known *exactly* how to respond to him. It wasn't something that happened instinctively with a first kiss. That knowledge only came with practice, and consciously, or unconsciously, Rachel had known what he'd wanted from her and how to give it to him.

A knock sounded and Trudy stuck her head in the door. "Are you two all right?" she asked.

"Yes," Reid said, walking back around his desk. "We're fine."

"May I come in?"

"Please," Rachel answered.

Her gaze locked with Reid's. Her eyes told him their talk had ended. His said yes . . . for now.

"If that's all . . ." Rachel said to him as she stood.

"May I call you?" he asked.

"I..." Rachel looked to Trudy, then back to Reid. "Yes, if you wish."

"I do."

"Fine."

"I'll go home with you," Trudy said, then turned to Reid. "Unless you need me for something?"

Reid shook his head. "No," he said as he walked the two women to the door, opened and held it for them.

Rachel turned to him, feeling ridiculously awkward. She held out her hand. "Goodbye...Reid."

"Thank you for coming," he said politely, and shook her hand.

His hand said one thing, his eyes another. Rachel wondered which message was for her. Perhaps both, she mused, and gave him a tentative smile as she left.

Reid stood in his doorway staring into space long after Rachel and Trudy departed. Charlotte studied him, waiting for him to say something. When he didn't, she resumed typing. The sound galvanized him and he pushed himself to move.

"Charlotte," he said as he turned to reenter his office. "Get Mazelli back on the phone."

Rachel's visit to the doctor confirmed what she already knew to be true. She spent the first week of August thinking. Options, she'd told Reid. Choices. There were many in this day and age, but for some reason, she felt hers were limited.

She was thirty years old. Not old, but not young, either. A perfect age, really, to take on the responsibilities of motherhood. If she had married Tom, this would have been just about the time they would be starting their family. But she hadn't married Tom. She hadn't married anyone. And there was no one on the romantic horizon.

A fleeting image of Reid James skipped through her mind and she quickly dismissed it. He didn't believe her, and she hadn't the will or the energy to convince him. Besides, she was fed up with having to work at making people want her...love her. And even if she had, Reid James would be the least likely candidate.

In her mind's eye she could still see the headline of the magazine article about him that Trudy had given her: New York's Most Eligible Bachelor. She winced. And he thought she wanted money from him. Ha! If she'd been that type of person, a quick call to the tabloids would bring her thousands. But that kind of notoriety was the last thing she wanted or needed.

No, there was no one but her in this picture, and whether or not Reid James wanted to be part of the decision-making process, first and last, the choice was hers.

She wanted the baby. It was really as plain and simple as that.

The other choices were not so simple. She still had most of the money her mother had left her, but it wouldn't last long without a job. As much as she loved New York, it was an expensive place to live, even if she did approach Reid for help.

And that she wouldn't do. Something deep inside warned her that if she allowed him in, he could, quite possibly, take over not only her life but the baby's, as well. Living in the afterglow of Reid James's spotlight didn't appeal to her, and it wasn't at all what she wanted for her child. She cherished her independence too much for that, and to keep it, her best choice would be to return to Ohio to live with her father.

Her stomach tightened with the thought. His remarriage only two months after her mother's death had driven a wedge between them. Though they'd reconciled and had come to terms with each other, there was still a certain amount of tension between them that would make it difficult for her to go back home.

Rachel sat on the edge of her bed and cradled her head in her hands, trying not to remember the harsh words she and her father had exchanged the day of his remarriage. She'd harbored so much resentment of his callous behavior, it had all burst forth that day, ruining everything, or so he'd said.

But she hadn't been able to stop herself. Her mother had suffered for two years before her death, and Rachel had willingly nursed her. She had always known that her mother and father's marriage was not one made in heaven, but her mother's sickness had brought out the worst in her father. He couldn't deal with the illness that hung over the house like a shroud, so instead, he'd spent as little time as possible there, leaving the burden of care to Rachel.

Not that she'd minded. She'd loved her mother with a fierce loyalty that had lasted until she'd breathed her final breath, and beyond. But Rachel had paid a price for that devotion. Tom's initial patience with pushing back the wedding date wore thin as one year became two, and finally he, too, found someone else to give him the attention he craved.

The day after her mother's funeral, he'd broken the news to her. He'd met someone else. He was in love and going to marry her. Rachel remembered the blow of her mother's death and Tom's desertion like a one-two punch at a heavyweight match. The final straw was when her father introduced her to his lady-friend, and told her that he and the woman were marrying and moving into their home.

Her mother's home.

It was all too much for Rachel. She'd exploded the day of his marriage, and the screaming fight that ensued left them both angry and shaken. At the time, the rift had seemed irrevocable as far as Rachel was concerned. She'd moved out that same day, staying with an old school friend and her husband until she could make arrangements to move away.

New York had been a big, sprawling refuge, a place to lose herself, a place to hide. But she'd found that hiding was not enough for her. She'd been sure her mother was watching over her when she'd landed the first job in the garment industry for which she'd applied. She'd apprenticed to a cloth designer, building on her fashion schooling, learning the fabric trade. She'd found an apartment, met Trudy, and had her life running on an even keel for the first time in a very long time.

And then the bottom fell out. She lost her job when the parent company made what they called "necessary cutbacks." Since she had been the last hired, she was the first fired. That was four months ago. She'd pounded the pavement ever since in hopes of landing a new job, substitute waitressing at the corner coffee shop during the lunch hour to supplement her meager inheritance.

Though her pride bristled at the thought of crawling back home, she knew that was her best course of action. At least if she wanted to have the baby. And she did. That was the only thing of which she was absolutely sure.

So the decision was made.

The buzzer sounded and Rachel rolled off the bed. Trudy had promised to stop by after work and bring take-out. Not that Rachel was the least bit hungry, but she knew if she didn't eat, Trudy would lecture her, and she would have to agree. She was, after all, now eating for two.

She hit the button and set the table with silverware and napkins as she waited for Trudy to arrive. As the knock sounded, Rachel opened the door to her friend standing with a shopping bag full of Chinese food.

"Did you buy out the restaurant?" Rachel asked with an indulgent smile.

"No, I didn't buy out the restaurant. I just bought enough for you to have some leftovers. I *know* you won't cook for yourself."

"You're impossible," Rachel said.

Trudy patted her cheek as she placed the shopping bag on top of the table. "But you love me anyway."

They sat down to eat, and Trudy smiled, her mouth stuffed with lo mein. "Don't we get along great?" she asked.

"Wonderfully," Rachel said as she toyed with the fried rice.

"You know," Trudy began, "we'd be great together."

"Together?"

"Yeah. Living together."

"What are you talking about?" Rachel asked.

"You. Me. Living together at my place."

"Oh, Trudy—"

"No, really. We could do it. I work all day. You could help me out keeping the place neat and all."

"Don't be ridiculous. You barely have enough room for yourself."

"That's not true. There's that little alcove. We could put the crib in there. You could sleep in my room."

"And what about Jake?"

"What about him?"

"Your relationship is just heating up. How is he going to fit into all this?" Rachel asked with a shake of her head. "Really, Trudy. Three's a crowd. And once the baby comes, it'll be four."

"So? We'll have a parade! Come on, we can do it."

Rachel shook her head. "No." She leaned forward and put her hand over Trudy's, not even trying to fight the tears that filled her eyes. "You are the best friend I've ever had in my entire life. Thank you for the offer, but no. I've already made up my mind what to do."

"And that is?"

Rachel pulled back her hand and looked down at her dinner. She didn't answer right away. She couldn't bring herself to say the words, as if once she did, she would be bound by them.

"Well?" Trudy prompted.

Rachel lifted her eyes and met her friend's concerned stare. "I'm going back home."

"You can't. You'll hate it there."

"I've already called the airlines."

"But have you called your *father?*"

"No. But I will. Tomorrow." She looked at Trudy's disapproving face. "I have no other choice."

"Yes, you do."

"What? Tell me what other choices I have?"

"Reid."

Rachel shook her head adamantly. "No."

"Why not? He's got more money than God. He can help you out, get you a job, set you up—"

"No. Don't even think it. I won't take money from him. Not now, anyway. Maybe later. When the baby's older. For college."

"Why? For heaven's sake, tell me, why?"

Rachel gave up on eating. She stood and scraped the remainder of the food off her plate into the trash. "Because I'd be putting myself—the baby—up for sale. I'd feel *obligated* to him. Not to mention the publicity. Can you imagine what the newspapers would do if they found out about this? New York's most eligible bachelor and *moi*. I could see the headlines now."

"You'd live through it."

"But I don't want to live through it! I want to have my baby in peace and quiet. I don't want to become part of any Reid James media circus. I couldn't do it, Trudy, even if he offered." She paused. "He hasn't, has he?" she asked.

Trudy shook her head slowly. "No, but I know he would if—"

"If I asked him? Oh, Trudy, can't you see how that would make me feel?"

Trudy got up from the table and came over to Rachel. She put her arm around her. "Why are you being so stubborn? He can do things for you."

"I think he's done enough for me already, don't you?"

"That's not fair," Trudy said. "He's really a great guy. A little rough around the edges, but that's to be expected based on his background."

"What about his background?"

The phone rang. Rachel drew a deep breath and let it out slowly as she walked over to answer it by the bed. She lifted the receiver.

"Hello?"

"Rachel? How are you?"

It was Reid. Rachel sank onto the edge of the bed and mouthed his name to Trudy. "Fine. I'm fine."

"I hope you don't mind my calling. Trudy gave me the number."

"No. No, I don't mind your calling."

"Hell, no," Trudy said out loud. "We were just talking about you.

Rachel shushed Trudy with a wave of her hand. "What can I do for you?"

"I'd like to meet with you . . . talk to you."

Rachel shut her eyes and pressed her lips together for a moment. "I've already made my decision, Reid."

He hesitated. "And . . ."

"And I'm going to keep the baby."

If she thought it really mattered to him, Rachel could have interpreted a note of relief in his intake of breath.

"I'm glad."

"Are you?" she asked.

"Yes. Very. Will you meet with me?"

"I don't know for what, Reid."

"To discuss how we're going to handle this."

"*We* aren't handling anything. I've decided to go back home."

"Home?"

"To Ohio."

"Oh. Is that definite?"

"Yes. All the arrangements are made," she lied.

Reid was silent for a long time. Rachel could almost feel the steam from his temper seeping through the phone. Her heart began to pound.

Finally he said, "I see. Well, then, I guess this is—"

"Goodbye." Rachel finished his sentence for him.

She hadn't thought this would be so hard. She didn't really know him at all. For all intents and purposes he was a stranger. Except for the outcome of their night together, they would probably have never met again. He'd only been a face in a dream to her, but meeting him again, seeing the dream come to life, walk, talk, touch her, was unbalancing to say the least.

He was real, and they had shared something special. She felt something for him she couldn't even put a name to.

The lump in her throat was growing larger and more prohibitive by the second. She wasn't sure how much longer she could continue to speak, so she thought it best to end this conversation as soon as possible.

"I have to go."

"Okay..." he said softly. But when she didn't hang up, he added, "Rachel? Are you still there?"

"Yes..." she squeaked.

"Will you let me know...when, and all..."

"Yes. Of course. Goodbye, Reid."

And this time she did hang up, cradling the phone and gripping the receiver long after the connection was broken.

"Well, that's that," Trudy said with a faint tinge of disapproving resignation.

"Yes," Rachel said. "It's over."

Three

It wasn't over. Not as far as Reid was concerned. Not by a long shot.

Rachel Morgan couldn't possibly believe that she could enter his life, drop this kind of bombshell in his lap, and then shoo him away like an annoying fly on a hot summer day.

He stared at the phone on his desk for the longest time after cradling the receiver. He'd stayed late at the office with no desire to go home and return to the scene of the crime, so to speak. He wanted to wallow for a while, a bit of self-indulgence he'd made it a point never to give in to anymore, but for some reason needed to sink down into right now.

So she was going home, she said. To Ohio, no less. Not that he had anything against Ohio. He had a very nice, profitable business there. He even visited now and then. But Ohio was not where he lived. He was here. In New York. And this is where he wanted her to be.

Especially now. Especially since she'd decided to keep the baby.

He couldn't believe how pleased—no, *overjoyed*—he was by her decision. Or how apprehensive he had been about what that decision might be. He didn't really know what he would have done if she had chosen otherwise, but he would have done something.

He wanted her in his life. In whatever capacity she'd accept, and that was the bottom line. He needed to come up with a strategy to accomplish that, and that would take some planning. But he was good at planning. He'd lived his whole life setting and reaching goals, most of them deemed by others to be impossible. This would be no different.

He would set her up. An apartment on the Upper West Side maybe. Something near the park so that they could take the baby there on nice days. He'd get her a nanny, or better yet, a nurse, too. The best of care for his son . . . or daughter. Whatever. It didn't matter. The child was his. No report from Mazelli was going to refute what he knew in his heart to be so.

Right or wrong, good or bad, Rachel Morgan and Reid James had made a baby that night.

He wasn't a religious man, and he didn't believe in fate. You made your own luck. But too much had happened, too many things had had to fall into place for this to be dismissed as coincidence.

So something had brought them together that night. Be it God, or the fates, or the stars in the universe, something beyond and more powerful than them had decreed that this should be, and his gut instinct told him that there had to be a reason for it.

He'd always trusted his gut instinct, even when logic had said no, even when people had thought him crazy, and never, ever, had he been wrong. He wasn't wrong now, either. Rachel and he had made a baby and, ego aside, he was meant to be part of the child's life.

So that meant one thing.

She wasn't going to live in Ohio.

And he'd have to work on the way to stop her.

He mulled over his options. He didn't know much about her, but what he did know told him she wouldn't take well to the authoritarian approach. No, she'd have to be gently persuaded, perhaps with a healthy dose of reality and logic.

But she had a tender side, too. His insides twisted with the memory of the warmth she was capable of. She said she didn't remember any of it, but *he* did, and that would have to do for now.

Reid tapped his index finger against his mouth as he contemplated his next course of action. His private line rang and he picked it up.

"Yes?"

"Mazelli, here. I've got something for you."

"That was fast."

"Once I had her name, it was a breeze, Mr. J. She's no mystery."

Easy for you to say. "Tell me."

"Thirty. Typical small-town background. School, church, you know the drill. Mother dead two years. She'd been sick a long time. Rachel nursed her to the end. Father remarried—"

"When?" Reid asked.

"Couple of months after the mother died."

"Interesting."

"Yeah. Real heartbroken guy."

"Anything more?"

"She was engaged to a Tom Walcott. Sold insurance. He broke it off and married someone else. Got a kid now." Mazelli paused. "From the dates, it looks like he left her around the time her mother died."

"Another sweetheart," Reid said, a picture beginning to form in his mind.

"Also," Mazelli continued, "she came to New York after that. Worked for Forster Fashions for a year and a half, then got laid off. She's currently unemployed except for a part-time deal with a local restaurant." When Reid was silent, Mazelli added, "The lady's had a lot of tough breaks."

"It would seem so. Anything else?"

"Nah. Just the usual. Address, phone number, credit rating—"

"Give me the address." Mazelli obliged.

"One other thing. She charged a one-way airline ticket to Ohio."

"For when?"

"The last Friday in August."

Reid marked his desk calendar. "That's the Friday of Labor Day weekend."

"Yep."

"Thanks. You do good work, Mazelli."

"Call me anytime, Mr. J."

"You got it."

Reid hung up and stared at the address he'd scribbled across the white pad. Ripping off the sheet of paper, he folded it and stuffed it in his shirt pocket. He lifted his jacket off the back of his chair and put it on, unconsciously straightening his tie and tugging at his French cuffs as he headed for the door.

The end of the month. That didn't leave him much time. But he worked under pressure all the time, and if nothing else, it spurred him on all the more.

He left Charlotte a note. He wouldn't be in tomorrow. Perhaps not the day after that, either. A feeling of elation washed over him with the realization that he'd found what he'd been looking for—a damned good reason for him to take a break from the business, a new challenge, something exciting, important.

A reason for living.

A baby and . . .

Rachel.

Everything was packed. When Rachel surveyed the meager display of boxes, she became even more depressed than she already was. When she'd first arrived in New York it had been smarter—and cheaper—to rent furniture for a while. The "while" became much longer than she'd ever imagined, and she'd never gotten around to purchasing anything worth taking.

The rental company had picked up the few pieces that had been part of her life these two years, leaving only these boxes filled with her personal items. Not much to show for her time here, she thought. So, apparently, did the moving company she'd hired. They were piggybacking her belongings with another family's, and she was more or less at their mercy.

So there she sat, on a box in the middle of her empty studio apartment waiting for the movers to arrive. She had planned to spend her last night in New York with Trudy, but she'd had to push up her departure date unexpectedly. She would have to leave this afternoon to accommodate her father's schedule. She and Trudy had had to make do with a tearful goodbye on the telephone this morning.

Most of all, she would miss her friend. Trudy represented all that was right about the city Rachel had adopted as her home. How would she survive without her wit and her wisdom? Rachel smiled to herself, remembering Trudy's last words. "Don't forget. You always have a home here with me."

But Rachel knew that once she left, she'd never return, not even for a visit. She wouldn't be able to handle it. Her stomach churned anew with the realization that in a few hours she would be back in her father's house.

It's funny, she thought, sometime during the two years she'd been away, the house she'd grown up in had ceased to be hers or even her mother's. It had become her father's house. Her father's and his wife, Sally.

It had been so hard making that phone call...

Shaking herself out of her reverie, Rachel bit her lip. *You're making the right decision,* she repeated to herself for the hundredth time.

She checked her watch. She still had time, but not much. Mentally, she shrugged. Even if the movers didn't arrive before she had to leave, she had arranged to have her super let them in.

The buzzer sounded, and with a sigh of relief Rachel rose and hit the entrance button. She opened her front door to allow them to enter, then made a quick and final foray around the large L-shaped room to check for the umpteenth time that she had packed everything.

Bent over a box, she heard the knock. "Come on in," she said. "Everything's ready to go."

"Rachel?"

She spun around at the sound of his voice. Reid stood in the doorway, dressed casually in low-riding jeans and a blue sport shirt, one hand on the knob, one foot over the threshold.

"Reid! What are you doing here?"

"May I come in?"

"Yes, of course." She straightened, running her fingers through her hair to smooth it back in place. "Moving day," she said with a sheepish grin and a hand motion toward the boxes.

"So I see." He shut the door behind him and moved more deeply into the room. "I've come in the nick of time."

"Nick of time? To what?"

"To persuade you not to go."

When Trudy had called to advise him that Rachel was leaving today and not Friday as originally planned, he'd jumped into his clothes and called for his car. Though he knew if he missed her he could just as easily follow her to Ohio, common sense told him that he would stand a better chance if he pleaded his case before she set foot on the plane. Once she was back home it would be more difficult to get her to return.

More difficult, but not impossible.

Rachel smiled. "I'm afraid it's too late for that. My plane leaves in—" she checked her watch again "—two hours."

"The plane can take off with or without you, Rachel."

"But it won't."

"Won't you at least hear me out before you leave?"

Rachel shut her eyes for a long moment. "Please don't do this, Reid. I've said all I have to say to you over the phone. This is difficult enough without you confusing the issue at the eleventh hour."

"Perhaps the fact that it's difficult is telling you something."

"Such as?"

"That you shouldn't go."

Rachel shook her head. "There are no other options."

"Yes, there are. You've chosen not to pursue them."

"You mean, you."

"Yes, me."

"No."

"Why not?"

"Because I'm not taking any money from you. I'm not... the baby's not for sale."

"I would never presume to think that. There are other ways, Rachel. Not money. Help. So that you don't have to go back to your father with your tail between your legs."

"How do you know about that?"

"I don't. I guessed."

"You had me checked out, didn't you?" she asked.

"Yes, I did. Things haven't been easy for you, have they?"

Unbidden tears tightened her throat and she fought for control. She stared at him. His eyes were an all-business green, cold, hard, deliberate. Why was he doing this?

"Why are you doing this?" she asked, the words tumbling out of her mouth.

"Because I want you to stay."

"What you mean is, you want the baby."

"Same thing."

"Not to me."

Reid's jaw tightened and he pinned her with his eyes. The words hung in the air as the buzzer sounded again. Rachel didn't move right away, mesmerized by his presence and his intense look. It buzzed again.

"I'd better get that." She walked around him and hit the button, then turned back to him. "The movers are here."

"Cancel them."

"I can't—"

"Yes, you can."

She shook her head. "No."

Reid came up to her and grabbed her by the shoulders. "Give me a chance to talk you out of this."

"The plane—"

"All right. My car is downstairs. I'll take you to the airport. If I can't change your mind before the plane takes off, I'll come back and personally arrange to have your belongings transported to Ohio. Deal?"

"Why would you—"

"The meter's ticking, Rachel. All I've got is two hours to convince you to stay. Give me at least this, won't you?"

The knock saved her from answering. A gruff voice sounded on the other side of the door. "Movers."

Reid's gaze locked with hers. She didn't protest when he pulled her back from the door and opened it. He took it for her acquiescence.

"We won't be needing you anymore," he said to the burly man standing in the hall.

"What? I got an order here says I have to pick up—"

"Yes, well, the order's canceled." Reid reached into his pocket and pulled out a billfold. Extracting one of the larger denominations, he handed it to the mover. "For your trouble."

The man looked at the bill, then at Reid. "Suit yourself," he said, then marched back toward the elevator mumbling to himself.

Reid shut the door and turned to face Rachel.

"Now you've done it," she said. "The way things were I already had to wait a week for my things. Now who knows when I'll see them again."

"I promise you'll have everything within a week if I have to rent a truck and drive to you myself."

Rachel turned her face from him, his eyes too penetrating for her to withstand right now. He was seeing too much with those eyes. Seeing things she didn't want to admit even to herself.

She hadn't realized how fragile she was until he'd appeared. She had thought she was handling this move so well. Why even the difficult phone call to her father had gone okay, with Sally being very congenial and friendly, and her father's voice soft and welcoming.

She'd thought she had reconciled herself to her decision to go home. She was no longer hesitant about leaving, had even convinced herself that it might be fun living back in her old room, seeing everyone again.

But she hadn't counted on Reid showing up and dredging up all her reservations she'd done her best to bury.

"I have to leave," she said, feeling trapped here in this small apartment with him and her misgivings.

Reid picked up her two suitcases. "I'll take you to the airport."

She nodded, following him out the door, locking it behind her. Rachel glanced at the key in her hand and was about to pocket it, then changed her mind. "Here," she said to Reid. "Take this. You'll need it to ship my stuff."

"I'll take it, but I won't need it," he said.

Her smile was puzzled. "You seem so sure you'll get your way."

Reid put a hand to her back and ushered her toward the elevator. "I usually do."

"Not this time," she said.

He leaned toward her, his face so close and so serious she could count those charming laugh lines around his eyes.

"Oh, Rachel, don't be so naive. *Especially* this time."

He escorted her out of the building and into his waiting limousine. The traffic was predictably heavy, but moving, as Reid's driver inched his way through the Midtown tunnel toward LaGuardia Airport. Rachel studied Reid out of the corner of her eye. They'd been in the car for fifteen minutes already and he'd yet to say a word.

Who was this man?

According to everything she knew about him, he had it all. He was rich, handsome, bright, and despite his inauspicious beginnings, respected. The newspapers and magazines made note of every woman he'd dated, never failing to mention that he'd never shown the slightest long-term interest in any of them.

She looked out the tinted window at the creeping traffic. She should never have told him about the baby, though at the time there had been no question in her mind that he'd had a right to know. But she'd never thought he'd want to be involved in any way.

He had a reputation for being cold and remote in relationships. Trudy had said it had to do with his being illegitimate and raised in an orphanage, and from what she'd read, that was probably true. Everything in his background said he was a loner, someone who eschewed commitment, someone who thrived on the chase, on the "getting there" rather than the end result.

The baby was the end result, and she had been convinced that he would make some token monetary offer that she would refuse and then he'd be gone from her life. But such was not the case. He'd even surprised Trudy, who claimed to know him so well, with his diligent pursuit.

What did he want from her?

She couldn't allow herself to become involved with him in any way. It would doom her, she could feel that in her bones. There was something seductive about him, something that beckoned her. When she was near him, he seemed to cast a spell over her. She acted differently, as if she'd lost control of her senses. He was charming and very convincing. It was probably that same something that had compelled her to go with him the night of the party. Alcohol or prescription drugs aside, consciously or unconsciously, she was extremely susceptible to him.

Which meant he could hurt her. And Lord help her, but she had been hurt so much in the last few years, she was notoriously self-protective. She had to fight this attraction to him, fight it with every fiber in her being, because if she didn't, she instinctively knew that the hurt this time would be beyond any she'd ever experienced, possibly beyond anything she could withstand. This time, there would be a baby to worry about.

This time, it would be devastating.

"Why do you think this happened?" he asked suddenly, as if he'd been reading her mind.

"I don't know. A mistake—"

"No. Don't use that word. There may be many reasons for this, but mistake isn't one of them."

"Okay. It wasn't a mistake. Then what was it?"

"I've spent a lot of time thinking about it. I go 'round and 'round, but the answer always comes up the same."

"And that is?" she asked.

His gaze locked with hers. "That perhaps it was meant to be."

"The baby?"

"Yes. The baby. But you, too. And me."

"Do you really think that, Reid? I don't."

"Then give me your reasons why."

She shrugged. "I don't know. These things just happen. It wouldn't be the first time. An accident—"

He took hold of her hand. "No. No accident, Rachel. I used a condom."

Her eyes widened. "You did?"

"Yes."

His touch was warm, solid, comforting. She pulled her hand away. "No wonder you were suspicious."

"Yes. At first I was. But no more."

"Why no more? Because you discovered how boring my life has been?"

He grinned. "No. I'd made up my mind before that. Let's just say, it felt right—" he tapped his chest "—in here."

"And that was enough for you?"

"If you knew me, you'd know that it's all I ever go by."

"But I don't know you. Not at all."

His eyes shone like emeralds. "You already know all that is important about me."

She was beginning to enjoy these little cryptic sentences he threw out at her every once in a while. She grinned with amusement. "And that is?"

"That I want you and the baby in my life. And that I will do anything in my power to make that happen."

"Even if I don't want it?"

"Ah, but that's the real question, isn't it? Have you really asked yourself what you want, Rachel?"

"Yes, I have. I want to be left alone to have and raise my child."

"Back home? Living with your father and his wife?"

"Okay. So it's not my first choice. But it's the only one that makes sense."

"Mine makes more sense."

"Yours is good for you and not for me."

"It can be good for both of us. But most of all, it's good for the child. Two parents are better than one."

"Women raise children alone all the time, Reid. This is the nineties."

"But it doesn't make it right."

She looked at him. "So what are you suggesting, Reid? Setting me up in an apartment? A nanny for the baby?"

"Initially, yes. I did think along those lines. But no more."

"So?"

Reid sat back in the seat. "I have a small house in Connecticut. A few miles inland from the Sound. I've never used it, haven't even been there in years, and almost forgot about it until Charlotte reminded me." He turned to look Rachel in the eye. "You have a fan, you know, in Charlotte."

"She seems like a very kind woman."

"Yes, she is. And savvy, too. Anyway, once she mentioned the house, I began to think that this would be a much better place to raise a child than an apartment in Manhattan." He turned to her. "I think you'd like it."

Rachel stared at him as the car stopped at her airline depot. She moved to get out of the car as the driver came around to open the door.

Reid held her wrist. "What do you say?"

"It's a generous offer, Reid, but no. I don't think it would work out."

"Why not?"

She hesitated. She couldn't very well tell him the truth: that she was scared to death of him, of the things he made her feel, of his power over her, of the crazy possibility that with the least little effort on his part, she could fall hopelessly, madly in love with him.

Instead she lifted her chin as she exited the car. "I can't take charity."

His face turned grim as he followed close behind. "What you mean is, you can't take charity *from me.*"

She shook her head at him. "I'm not taking charity. I'm going back home to live with my father."

"Your father and his *wife,*" Reid clarified.

That stung. He knew too much about her. Rachel threw him a withering look. "Yes. My father . . . and his wife."

Rachel handed a skycap her airline ticket and stood still as he wrapped baggage claim tickets around her luggage.

Reid ran a hand through his hair. She was the most exasperating woman he had ever met. What was wrong with her? Didn't she understand that his idea was the best for both of them, the best for the baby? How could she want to live back home in what had to be an impossible situation for her? Well, he wasn't about to give up now. Or ever.

She turned from the skycap and extended her hand. "Thank you, Reid, for the ride and the offer, but I have to be going."

He took her hand, but didn't let go. "I haven't finished."

"Yes, you have," she said as she turned and walked into the terminal.

Reid muttered an expletive and told his driver to park the car. He ran to catch up with her as she stood in the line to go through the metal detector, excusing his way past a gaggle of people none too happy with his pushy manner. But there was no time for niceties now. In a few minutes she would be on the plane and he would have lost his chance to plead his case.

God, how he hated to lose.

He caught up with her as she walked quickly to her gate. As he grabbed her arm, she turned and rolled her eyes to heaven.

"Reid—"

"I know. I'm not doing a very good job explaining this. What I'm trying to say is that the house is big enough for us to comfortably share it. I want to be around to see this child grow, Rachel. I don't want to be a check in the mail and a weekend 'Uncle Daddy.'"

"What are you saying, Reid? You want to *live* with me and the baby?"

"In a manner of speaking."

"What manner?"

"Whatever you'll allow."

"You can't imagine I'd be *kept* like some high-class mistress."

"I don't want you to be my mistress, Rachel. What I'm saying is that I don't want to have to make an appointment to see my child. I want to be there. All the time. And there's only one acceptable way to do that."

"And that is?"

"What I want, Rachel, is for you to be my wife."

Her mouth fell open. "You're insane." She shook her head as if to clear it, turned and began walking once again to her assigned gate.

"No, I'm not."

The voice behind her in the boarding line was familiar and persistent. She ignored it.

"I said, I'm not crazy. I know exactly what I'm doing."

She looked at him over her shoulder. "Do you really?"

"Yes."

She stopped. "Then tell me why you want to marry me."

Reid pulled her out of the line. "Because it will solve all our problems," he said, the gleam back in his eye now that he had her attention again.

"You mean, it will solve all your problems, not mine."

"Who are you thinking of, Rachel? Yourself or the baby?"

"Both. I'm willing to make sacrifices for my child, Reid, but not ones that will affect how I live, how I feel. If I'm not happy, the baby won't be happy, either."

"And you think you'll be unhappy married to me?"

She laughed and nodded. "Yes, I do. We don't even know each other. You and I are from different worlds. I would never fit into yours, nor would I want to. You may be doing this out of some warped sense of ego, but believe me, this child means more to me than a bargaining chip."

The last passengers boarded the plane and the flight attendant made the last call.

"This has nothing to do with my ego."

"Reid, please let it go. I won't come back with you. I won't live with you. I won't marry you. I'm flattered, believe me, but this just won't work. We don't even know if we like each other. I'm sorry to disappoint you. But you can't just *will* something to happen."

Rachel turned from him, tears threatening. She had to get away from him. The urgency of the message was registering in every nerve in her body. He was too strong, too compelling, too used to getting his own way. My God, he'd even gone to the lengths of proposing marriage! A marriage, she was sure he had no intentions in the world of going through with. The man was obsessed, and she could not—would not—allow herself to get caught up with him.

He took hold of her arm as the flight attendant urged her forward. "Please. I have to go."

"Rachel, give me one more—"

"No. No more. Think about it, Reid . . . and ask yourself a question—would you be proposing marriage if I wasn't pregnant?" He opened his mouth to speak, but she put up her hand to stop him. "No, think first about what I've asked. And while you're at it, think about this, too. What happened between you and me *was* a mistake. Accept it."

She pulled her arm away and almost ran through the plane's entrance portal.

Reid stood back as the flight attendant shut the door. He walked to the window and watched the lights blink on the plane as it pulled away from the terminal.

He could not accept it.

Nor did he need to think about it.

He didn't believe in mistakes.

Ever since he could remember, he'd been told that *he'd* been a mistake. He didn't accept it then and wouldn't believe it now.

No, Rachel, you're wrong.

This was no mistake.

I won't let it be.

Four

Rachel sat across the dinner table from a smiling Sally.

"What are you planning to do tomorrow, Rachel?" Sally asked as she passed the green beans.

"Better start looking for a job," Al Morgan said before Rachel could answer.

"I intend to, Dad."

"Not as easy as you think," Al continued. "The unemployment rate is higher here than in the city. You're just not gonna walk into a place and get what you want."

"I'll find something."

"I hope so."

"I'm sure she will, Al," Sally said, patting Al's hand.

They exchanged a look, then both smiled at her. Her father's smile was strained, but Rachel returned it anyway. He was trying. They both were. She told herself that was all that mattered. She had known this would be difficult and awkward for all of them. But she had been home for less than a week and already her nerves were fraying.

She had forgotten how argumentative he was. He didn't mean anything by it; it was an integral part of his personality. He had something to say about everything and always had to have the last word. While her mother had been healthy, she had borne the brunt of it. During the time her mother had been sick, he had pretty much left the two women in his life to their own devices.

So, in fact, it had been years since Rachel had had to deal with him directly, and like an avalanche, the memories of those difficult childhood times came back to haunt her. Her already-nauseous stomach churned.

She put down her fork.

"Aren't you going to eat some more?" Sally asked, inching the plate toward Rachel.

"No, thanks, Sally. I'm not very hungry."

"You don't eat enough. You're skin and bones."

"She looks fine to me," her father said.

Rachel pushed back the chair and excused herself. "I think I'll take a shower and turn in early," she said.

"Don't use all the hot water." Her father's voice followed her as she left the room.

Rachel gripped the newel post on the banister and shut her eyes tightly. This was going to be a lot harder than she'd thought. These last few days seemed like weeks, and she longed for the quiet and privacy of her small apartment. She tried as best she could to stay out of everyone's way, but the house was small and sounds traveled. At night she could hear Sally and her father's frantic whispering in the room across the hall. It didn't take a genius to figure out that she was the main subject.

And she hadn't even *told* them yet.

They were under the impression that she was returning home because she'd lost her job, and to date, Rachel had not expounded on that belief. She had planned to break the news about the baby when she'd arrived, but her father's welcome had been genuinely warm and she hadn't wanted to do or say anything that might spoil it.

Since then, there hadn't been what she would call "the right time" to bring it up, though yesterday as Rachel had helped with the laundry, Sally had shown her willingness to engage in a little "girl talk." Rachel had almost blurted it out then, but the phone had rung and the moment was lost.

Surprisingly, Rachel liked Sally. She hadn't expected to. In fact, she had expected to greatly *dislike* the woman who had taken her mother's place so effortlessly. But Sally was sweet, kind, and totally without malice. She'd gone out of her way to make Rachel feel at home, here in the house in which she'd been raised.

But no matter how hard Sally tried, Rachel felt like an intruder. The house hadn't changed all that much. Rachel had. In the two years she'd been away, she'd made drastic changes in her life. She'd become less fearful, more independent, and had learned to *like* herself more than she ever had prior to living alone.

She didn't like herself now, not the way she was acting with her father. And it was an act. The problem was that it could become habit if she wasn't careful.

Rachel slowly climbed the steps, gathered her robe and undergarments, and walked into the bathroom. She locked the bathroom door behind her and flipped on the shower. The room quickly filled with steam and she glanced at her reflection as she stripped.

Her body hadn't changed yet, but she felt the portent of things to come. Her breasts were fuller, more sensitive, and the slight roundness of her tummy wouldn't go away when she sucked in her breath. She hugged her arms around herself and allowed the warm, misty air to embrace her like a lover's arms.

Instantly Reid's face appeared in her mind's eye the way he'd looked that night—in her dream that was no longer a dream but a reality that haunted her with increasing frequency since he'd stepped back into her life.

She thought about him all the time now, and even her best excuses for that fact couldn't wash away the feelings she'd acquired for him in the short time they'd been together. She tried to put him out of her head, but her heart wouldn't let her. There was something so urgent in his message to her, something deeper than the fact that he wanted to be part of the baby's life.

Rachel wished she knew more about him, beyond the superficial, published accounts of his life that Trudy had given her. Details of his climb to the pinnacle of the business world had all been there in the article, but they hadn't touched on the man, who he was, what he was, what went on inside his head, his soul.

That was what intrigued Rachel. The man inside. The impulsive man who was willing to ask her to marry him to get what he wanted. He wanted the baby, that was clear, and based on the fact that he himself was illegitimate and orphaned, she supposed it wasn't surprising that he didn't want a child of his to be even partially tarred by the same brush. But the mores of today were different from those of thirty-plus years ago, so there was really no need to offer marriage.

She'd had time to wonder about that proposal. What would he have done if she'd accepted? Probably pass out. Or, more likely, play the game with her for a while until she was committed to stay in New York. She couldn't bring herself to believe he had been serious.

But what if he had been...

A knock at the door started her out of her reverie. "Almost done?"

"Almost, Dad," Rachel said, quickly slipping into the shower.

She soaped up, rinsed down and dried off in record time. Throwing on a terry robe, she grabbed her underwear and opened the door to find her father standing in the hallway. "Sorry," Rachel murmured before hurrying off to her old bedroom.

She shut the door and sank onto the edge of the bed to towel-dry her hair. A light breeze blew in through the open window. Rachel lifted her face to it. She dropped the towel and ran her fingers through her hair as the air dried it. For the longest time she sat there staring out at the setting sun through the rustling leaves of the old oak tree she'd climbed as a child. Though after seven, it was still light, these first days of September clinging hopelessly to what was left of summer.

Sounds from the street drifted up to her: the distant buzz of a lawnmower, a children's game of hide-and-seek, the after-dinner lingering of a Labor Day barbecue from a neighbor's backyard.

Suddenly her intention of spending the evening with a book in bed was not half so appealing.

Her ears pricked with the sounds of Sally and her father whispering in the room across the hall, and the decision seemed to make itself. She needed to get away from here, if only for a short walk in that world below. Rachel slipped out of her robe and donned her undergarments as she picked out a blue linen blouse and denim wraparound skirt from her closet.

She hesitated in the hallway outside her room debating whether or not to tell her father and Sally she was leaving, then decided she wouldn't be gone long enough for it to matter. Like a thief in the night, she tiptoed down the staircase and made it out the front door without a sound.

The air was cooler than she'd expected. Rachel told herself she would be wise to go back in for a sweater. But wise

or not, she was loath to do so and chose instead to be cold.
And free.

It had been a long time since he'd driven anything as cumbersome as a van. Reid shifted in the seat, adjusting his weight into the best possible position, but no matter how hard he tried, he couldn't get comfortable. He was spoiled. But then, he told himself, riding in the back of limousines will do that to you.

Trailers on the interstate whizzed by him in a blur. The van shook with the vibration, and he had to grip the steering wheel tightly to steady the vehicle. He almost missed the turnoff, muttering a string of particularly virulent expletives as he took his life in his hands and cut across two lanes to make the exit.

Reid blew out a sigh of relief. He didn't want to entertain the thought of what would happen if he'd missed it. The map was open and lay haphazardly across his lap. He had meticulously etched out a route in black marker that would bring him directly into Rachel's hometown. He figured once he was there, finding her house would be a piece of cake. After all, how big could the town be?

Big enough, he discovered as he drove up and down one avenue after another before ending up back at the strip mall adjacent to the interstate entrance. He forced himself to take a break, and checked into the motel across the road. No matter what happened with Rachel, he wasn't starting the return trip tonight.

After freshening up, he pocketed the room key and headed back toward the van. It was getting late, with darkness only an hour or so away. The gas station at the corner tempted him, but Reid decided to give his instincts one more chance before asking for directions.

Sometimes his tenacity surprised even himself. His first emotion after Rachel had departed on the plane was anger.

Who did she think she was? But he'd been working on controlling his impulse to rage, and while he still didn't suffer fools gladly, he had learned that anger was a useless, self-defeating emotion that sapped his energy. Energy better used to get what he wanted.

So he'd returned to the city and rented a van, loaded Rachel's belongings, bought a map and set off for Ohio. He could have had someone do this for him. Or he could have had his driver make the delivery while he flew out. But neither way seemed quite right. It was something *he'd* wanted to do, as if it meant earning a special badge of courage to go and bring her back himself.

And he meant to bring her back. This whole delivery trip was a charade as far as he was concerned, an excuse to come to her, to talk to her again. This time, he would do a better job of explaining himself. This time, she would respond to him the way he'd imagined.

He'd been fantasizing a lot about her since she'd stepped on that plane, and at some point in the fantasy she'd taken on a new and different persona. No longer was she the desirable woman from the party, nor the cunning, fortune hunter, nor Trudy's trustworthy friend. She'd become something else, something unimaginable only weeks ago. She'd become his.

His woman.

He couldn't pinpoint exactly when he'd begun thinking of Rachel that way, but the thought was now lodged in his mind. It must have also shown on his face. Charlotte had grinned knowingly when he'd told her his mission, but Trudy had thought he was crazy and said so. "If Rachel's gone home, she'll stay there. There's nobody more stubborn."

Yes, there was, he decided, wondering how much of this was in retaliation for being told he couldn't do it and how much was because he wanted a second chance to plead his case.

The only thing he didn't wonder about was his motive.

True, he'd had a strange start in life and because of it, a dysfunctional, disconnected childhood. He'd come to terms with that, taking with a grain of salt all the psychological mumbo-jumbo that had been applied to him over the years.

But despite his reluctance to agree with any of it, he had to admit that for the first time in his life he did feel *connected.* As corny as it sounded, Rachel carried part of *him* inside her. He couldn't let go, didn't want to, and wouldn't give up until he succeeded in getting her and the child into his life. The fact that he had tunnel vision when it came to Rachel told him something about his feelings for her. Something he wasn't sure he was ready to deal with.

So he was taking one step at a time right now, and first, he had to find her father's house. He slowed down, rolling past the stop sign and through the intersection as he checked the numbers on the houses.

Rachel paid no mind to the blue van other than to stop at the curb and wait for it to pass. When it didn't, she stepped down to cross the street and head back into the house. She was more than startled when the van made the turn into her driveway.

"Oh!" It stopped on a dime, and Rachel's gaze connected with the driver's. "Reid!" she exclaimed as he jumped out of the van. "What are you doing here?"

"Fulfilling a promise," he said as he flipped open the back door to the van to reveal the stack of boxes with her belongings.

Rachel couldn't believe how glad she was to see him. She couldn't believe how her heart was pounding, nor could she believe the feeling of utter elation that washed over her.

Hundreds of thoughts ricocheted through her mind as her eyes drank her fill of him. He looked incredibly handsome, even though his hair was tousled and his shirt hung half in, half out of his wrinkled jeans. Her insides twisted with a bittersweet ache as if the child, too, was as happy to see him as she. She fought a desire to reach out and touch him. He was so tall, so tanned, so masculine, so. . . *here.*

Reid stood still as she looked him over. He looked her over, too. The tilt of her chin, the smoky gray of her eyes, the rigidity of her stance made her look strong and fragile at the same time. He wished she'd open her arms to him, let him hug her, give in to a simple, friendly embrace. He didn't want more than that, not now. Just some minimum form of social contact that would nurture this profound need of his to touch her. The strength of it surprised him, and he had to splay his hands on his thighs to stop them from reaching for her.

And then their eyes met. There was warmth there... welcome. Reid felt the tension drain out of him. When he'd jumped in the van to make this trip, he'd given little thought to what reception he would find on the other end. He hadn't wanted to think that she might be angry or annoyed. Yet in the last few hours on the road, it hit him that that just might be the case. The relief he felt was tangible, and he ran a hand through his hair to cover any display of emotion.

"You look tired," Rachel said softly.

"I drove straight through."

"You didn't have to do this."

He gave in, reached over and ran a finger down the side of her cheek. "Yes, I did." Then he smiled.

The smile brought it all back to her. The crinkling green eyes, the blond hair falling across his forehead. She was just about to give in to the urge to touch him and push the thick strands of hair back from his face when she heard her father's voice.

"Rachel? Who's there?"

"A friend, Dad. He's brought my stuff from New York."

Al Morgan opened the front screen door and carefully descended the cement steps one at a time. Reid extended his hand as he approached the van, prepared for whatever reaction the man decided was appropriate. He was Rachel's father, and under the circumstances, he had the right to chew Reid up and spit him out if he chose to do so.

The two men shook hands as Rachel made the introductions. "Well, that's very nice of you, coming all this way for Rachel," Al said, eyeing both of them speculatively.

"Rachel is very special to me," Reid said simply.

"Is she now?" Al responded with a glance back to his daughter.

"Why don't we get these boxes inside?" she suggested, quickly putting an end to her father's speculation.

"Sure," Reid said, more than happy for the reprieve as well as eager to get the job done so that he could have some time alone with Rachel.

He lifted a box, as did Al Morgan. "Why don't you hold the door," Reid said to Rachel.

"Oh, she's no shrinking violet," Al said as he hoisted the heavy box into his arms and headed for the house. "She can handle a box or two herself."

Reid spun around to look at Rachel, who was showing an inordinate amount of interest in the color and texture of the van carpeting. He dropped the box onto the floor of the van, and turned her chin toward him. "Look at me," he said, and she did. "You haven't told him, have you?"

Rachel averted her gaze. "I will."

"When?"

"Soon."

"How soon? When you start showing?"

"Before that."

"Why haven't you told him already?"

"I couldn't, that's all."

"Why?"

"You don't understand!" she said, exasperated at his persistence.

"You're right. I don't." He pushed the box back inside and shut the van door. "But I will. Let's go."

Reid took hold of her arm and escorted her around to the passenger side of the van. He opened the door.

"What are you doing?" she asked as he boosted her up into the seat.

"Getting you away from here."

"My father—"

"I'll tell him," he said as he shut the van door.

Rachel watched as Reid approached her father who was coming back out of the house. She watched them exchange words, and nodded toward her father as his eyes searched and met hers. He shrugged and turned to go back inside.

"Where did you tell him we were going?" she asked as Reid climbed into the driver's seat.

"For coffee," he said as he pulled out of the driveway. "To talk and catch up on old times." He gave her a tight grin that looked more like a grimace.

"Where are we really going?" she asked as they picked up speed and headed out of the residential area of town toward the main highway.

He didn't answer. Within minutes he pulled the van into the parking lot of the motel.

"You've got to be kidding," Rachel said when he parked.

Reid took the keys out of the ignition and turned to her. "I have a room. I'd like you to come up."

"What for?" She eyed him skeptically.

"What do you think?" he asked with a smirk on his face.

"I don't know. That's why I'm asking."

He leaned forward. His face was only inches from hers. "I want to talk to you. In quiet. Where we won't be disturbed. This seemed like the best place." When she still seemed reluctant, he added, "I promise to keep both feet on the floor at all times."

"I'm not worried about that," she said.

"Then what are you worried about?"

Rachel bit her lip. Trouble was, she wasn't worried at all. What she was, was excited. She hadn't been alone with him—truly alone with him—since that night they'd been together. And she didn't remember that, not all of it, anyway.

She still wasn't over the shock of seeing him pull into her driveway. She felt herself shake inside as she looked into those clear green eyes.

"Okay?" he asked.

She nodded. "Okay."

The room was dark, cool, and relatively clean for a truck stop. Rachel walked over to the corner and sat down on a gray chair as Reid clicked on the lamp beside the double bed.

Reid turned to her. "Now, tell me what's going on," he said. "Why haven't you told your father about the baby?"

"The timing wasn't right."

"What does that mean, Rachel?"

"It means I couldn't tell him. Not yet. We're getting along. Everything is going okay. I don't want to ruin it."

"And telling him about the baby will *ruin* it?"

Rachel shook her head. "You don't understand. My father and I don't have the best relationship."

"I know that."

Her chin came up. "Oh, your investigation. Of course. Save me some breath then, Reid. What else do you know about me?"

"I know facts, not details."

"Like?"

"Like that the last few years haven't exactly been a picnic for you. Your mother was sick, and you nursed her. Your father remarried soon after."

She felt her throat tighten. "If you know all that, then you know about Tom, too."

"The insurance salesman? Yeah. The jerk dumped you."

Rachel dismissed his evaluation with a wave of her hand. "He didn't dump me. We grew apart. There was nothing there anymore. He met someone else. Tom was right to call it off..."

"But..."

"But my father didn't think so. He was angry when the engagement was broken. He'd counted on my marrying and moving out so that he and Sally could have the house alone. My change of plans put a crimp in his."

Reid remained silent. Rachel looked at him; his gaze was intense. Her stomach clenched with the sour memories. She stood and began to pace before continuing. "I couldn't believe he could be so callous. My mother had been so sick..." Rachel paused. "We argued." She bit her lip as tears threatened. "He said some *horrible* things. I did, too."

Rachel swallowed, but she couldn't stop the tears. They fell in rivulets down her cheeks. Embarrassed, she wiped at them with the backs of her hands, but once begun, there seemed to be no amount of effort able to stop them. "Oh, God!"

Reid covered the space between them in a split second. He pulled her to him and wrapped his arms around her. At the feel of his arms enfolding her, Rachel dissolved into uncontrollable sobs.

"It's okay," he said softly. "Go ahead, let it out."

And she did.

She couldn't remember ever losing control like this, ever crying like this, not even when her mother had died. It was as if all the anguish, all the grief, all the pain of the last few years had been tightly bottled up inside her and now burst forth. Why the sight, sound and feel of Reid James should trigger these pent-up emotions was more than her mind could handle.

Reid held her against his chest as he led them to the bed. "Shh," he said as he sank against the headboard and cradled her against him.

Rachel sobbed into his shirt for a long time. And then she got the hiccups. Feeling a tenderness he hadn't known he'd had in him, Reid smiled at the childlike reaction, pushed the errant strands of hair away from her face and kissed the top of her head.

Gradually, Rachel calmed down and her breathing gentled. Yet she didn't move away. Reid was in no hurry to let her go. He hadn't expected this, but understood the need for emotional release. He'd had his times when the only thing left for him to do was rage, and he'd learned how destructive that was to him as well as all around him. No, it was better to cry it out, and he was only too glad to help her, if helping her meant she would have a clear head when it was over.

They lay together for a long time, long enough for the light through the crack in the draperies to fade to darkness. Rachel knew she should extricate herself from his hold, but he felt too good, and it had been such a long time since someone had comforted her. Her eyelids became heavy, and she began to drift off, the emotional outburst taking a physical toll. Just as her eyes shut, she heard and felt his voice vibrate against her ear.

"You said something to me the day you left," he began in a low, serious tone. "You said, 'if I'm not happy, the baby won't be happy, either.' Tell me, Rachel. Are you really happy with this arrangement? Do you think you'll be happier here seven months from now? A year?" He rested his chin on the top of her head. "Why not give that time to me? You can always come back home."

Rachel lifted her tear-stained face to him. "What are you saying?"

He looked down at her. With his thumb, he wiped away a lone drop from the corner of her eye. "I meant what I said at the airport. Marry me, Rachel. Stay with me. Let me help you. For the baby's sake if not for yourself. At least until the baby's born. If you want to leave after that, I won't stop you."

"You mean, a divorce?"

"If that's what you want."

"How do I know you're not just saying this to get me to come back with you to New York?"

"I give you my word." He paused. "I'll even put it in writing."

She looked at him and opened her mouth to speak, but no words came out. Reid couldn't resist the picture she made with her face a mask of wonder and confusion, and her eyelashes spiked with tears. His head descended and he brushed his lips against hers. "Oh, Rachel . . ."

He took her mouth whole. With no preliminaries, his tongue swept into her mouth and explored its inner recesses so thoroughly, her head fell back against his arm for support. She whimpered, and then timidly touched her tongue to his. A bittersweet ache shot through his groin like a red-hot arrow at the contact, arousing him with alarming speed and accuracy. He scrunched down onto the pillows, taking her with him as he rolled to his side and brought them to the center of the bed.

Rachel reached up and cupped the back of his neck, running her fingers through the long hair at his nape. Reid lifted his mouth long enough to change angles, to taste her from this side, from that, losing himself, his reason, his ability to respond to anything except her, the smell of her, the deeply satisfying taste of her.

This was the kind of kiss he'd dreamed of since the night they'd been together, since that day in his office when that kiss taken in frustration had only whet his appetite for more. So much more. And here she was, alone with him the way he'd imagined it. He wanted to devour her, absorb her into himself, make her part of him, so deeply a part that she'd never question who or what she was to him, so deeply that she'd never want to leave....

When Reid broke away, Rachel's eyes were glazed. She was confused, battling a gamut of emotions from A to Z. His body was so tight, so hot, he knew beyond the shadow of a doubt what would happen if he took advantage of that confusion. In seconds, they could very easily be making love.

And afterward she wouldn't even be sure how it happened.

Uh-uh. Not again. The next time they made love—and as God was in heaven, there was most definitely going to be a next time—she would know with whom, what, when, why, and where she was making love. As much as he wanted her right now, he wanted that realization more.

Reid moved back to give her breathing space. He kissed the tip of her nose. "Don't answer me now, Rachel. Think about what I've said." He gently pushed her head back against his chest.

"Reid?"

"Not now. Rest."

Rachel shut her mouth and sighed. The heat of his kiss had left her drained, washed out...washed clean. Her mind was a jumble, but her spirit was soaring somewhere out there in a world she couldn't describe and didn't dare name. No one had ever affected her like this. Reid was intoxicating, as lethal as any mixture of drugs and alcohol could ever be. She felt a calmness descend upon her like a warm blanket, a feeling completely incongruous to what it should be under the circumstances.

She should move, do something about this. . . .

Her eyes drifted closed in an attempt to clear her mind. But it was not so easy in the position she was in. Everything around her was Reid. The feel of him, the smell of him, the sound of his heartbeat against her ear. . . .

Her body sank more fully into his, and Reid knew the moment she fell asleep. His hand at her waist slipped lower as she did and he gave in to a need to gently palm her still-flat belly. "Hello, baby," he whispered as he massaged the soft flesh beneath her denim skirt.

Reid leaned his head back against the pillow. He was tired and his emotions were rubbed raw. He shut his burning eyes for just a moment and tried to think of the next tack he would take with her if, after this, she still refused to return with him. He was reaching the end of the line, he knew. There was nothing more to offer her from a material point of view and not much more with which to appeal to her morally.

He could still feel her resistance to him. She didn't trust him. And why should she? She'd had it stuck to her by better people than him, and she knew it. Yet it was so inconceivable to him that he could lose this fight, this one that could turn out to be the most vital one of all, even more important than the one with his parents.

There had to be something else he could do. Some *something* that would change her mind, that would make her see that he was right, that this could work out for her, for him . . . for the baby. He clutched the material of her denim skirt in his fist and held tightly, and then, slowly, gently, he, too, drifted into sleep.

When Rachel opened her eyes, it was dark, with only the dim bulb of the bedside lamp lighting the room. Disoriented, she lifted her head. Her tongue peeked out of her mouth and wet her dry lips. She attempted to sit up but something was holding her back. Reid's hand. It was splayed across her abdomen, his fingers entangled with the front flap of her skirt.

Slowly, she tilted her head to look up at him. His head was at an odd angle and his eyes were closed in a much-needed deep sleep. Rachel inched herself away from him carefully so as not to wake him. Besides, she needed the space. The heat of his body was as overpowering as the heat of his mouth, and she needed time to think.

Rachel walked to the door and silently turned the knob. Night air greeted her as she stepped over the threshold onto the concrete deck of the motel. She shut the door behind her, but not completely, and took a deep breath. It was late, and she should be returning to her father's house. He'd be worried, concerned, or worse, and she had no desire to have to spend the remainder of the evening making excuses.

Reid had made a good point when he'd thrown her words back at her. Truth be told, she wasn't happy here living with her father. It wasn't even the old animosity from her mother's death anymore. She'd come to accept Sally and her father living in her childhood home. No, it was the fact that she'd found a new life in New York, a life that she liked, a life that she knew she would always miss.

Rachel lifted her face to the stars and allowed herself a wry grin. This, she assumed, was what was meant by "you can't go home again."

The door behind her swung inward. "Oh," Reid said, running a hand across his day-old stubble. "I thought you'd left me..." He trailed off, the word "again" hanging between them.

"No," she said, brushing past him as she reentered the room. "I was just getting some air." She turned to him. "And thinking."

Reid's antenna went up, and his gaze locked with hers. "Thinking?"

"Yes," she said.

"About?"

"My father, mostly. And what you said."

Reid was going crazy. He had no idea what this was leading to, but he could feel a renewal of adrenaline pumping through his veins. He walked over to the end table, lifted his pack of cigarettes, and tapped one out.

He lit it. "And?" When she didn't answer him right away, he glanced up at her through the haze of smoke. "Rachel? I asked—"

"You should quit," she said matter-of-factly.

His eyes narrowed, and he studied her for the longest time before answering. "I will."

"When?"

"One of these days."

"And when will that be?"

"What's it to you?"

She shrugged. "Nothing. It's just so unhealthy."

What was she getting at? "For?"

"You."

"Only me."

"And everyone around you."

Reid held the cigarette out in front of him and examined it from end to end. Then he looked at her and smiled. "Marry me, Rachel, and I'll quit."

Rachel laughed and shook her head. "You never give up, do you?"

"Never."

"What if I took you up on it?"

"Say yes and find out."

They stared at each other for the longest time with big grins on their faces. Slowly, Rachel's smile faded, as in turn did Reid's. His eyes roamed her face as he read the turmoil of her mind in her beautiful gray eyes. But he didn't speak. He couldn't. The ball was in her court. She'd brought it up. She'd allowed it to continue. She'd set the stage.

His heart was pounding like a man facing the foreman of his jury. This was it, and he knew it. Defiantly, he lifted the cigarette to his mouth and took a long drag. He released the smoke and watched it drift into the air.

"Come on, Rachel. Say it," he taunted.

The gauntlet dropped, the decision was made.

Rachel walked over to him. As if she were touching the most gross thing in the world, she picked the cigarette out from between his fingers and ground it into the ashtray.

When Rachel turned to face him, the realization of what she had done hit her right between the eyes. Her pulse began to race, and her mouth ran dry. Reid's face broke into a slow, knowing grin, and his crinkling eyes said it all.

He moved toward her. Rachel put out her hand to stop him. "A year, Reid. I'll try it for a year. Till after the baby's born."

"Whatever you say," he said with a triumphant smile.

He lifted her chin with his fingers and stared into her eyes for the longest moment. Rachel was frozen to the spot, unable to move even if she wanted to, which she did not. Then he brushed his lips ever so lightly against her lips, her cheek, the soft spot below her ear, where he paused only long enough to whisper, "Let's go home."

Five

It was a simple ceremony.

Rachel wore a pale mauve suit with a matching wide-brimmed hat that Trudy had insisted she buy. She and Reid stood side-by-side before a judge in his chambers and exchanged their vows.

It all seemed surreal to Rachel, as if this were happening to someone else and she was hovering overhead, somewhere in the vicinity of the center of the vaulted ceiling, observing instead of participating in the ritual. Reid's attorney, Jules Laraby, served as best man, a last-minute, expedient measure since he'd had an early morning meeting with Reid anyway.

The week after she returned to New York with him had been so rush-rush, hush-hush that Rachel felt as if she were moving in slow motion, the only live-action character in a cartoon movie. Beginning with the quick trip to the doctor for blood tests, the endless line at city hall for the license, right through Trudy's thorough department-by-department foray through Bloomingdale's, it had seemed to Rachel as if everyone involved was running to and fro with their best faces on, pretending, she was sure, that this was a happy, festive event.

When she said "I do," Reid kissed her, a disappointing, anticlimactic, perfunctory kiss that did nothing to inspire any confidence in her that this union would evolve into anything more than what it already was: a sham.

"Ready?" Reid asked after they'd signed the appropriate papers and shaken hands with the judge.

"Yes," she answered, allowing him to usher her from the chambers and out of the courthouse where an enterprising young photographer covering a trial recognized Reid and managed to snap a few frames of the two of them fleeing down the steps and into a waiting limousine.

Her hands were shaking. Rachel gripped the small bouquet of lavender-tinged orchids in an attempt to gain control. Reid turned to her and smiled. "Okay?" he asked, and she nodded.

But she was not okay. She was desperate to be anywhere but here. What had she gotten herself into? Why had she ever agreed to this? Right now she couldn't imagine a worse predicament. A picture formed in her mind. She saw herself bound, trussed up and tied down, unable to move. She gasped for air.

Trudy sat facing her. Reaching across, she gave Rachel's hand a squeeze. The two women's eyes met, and Rachel did her best to return a small smile to Trudy's beaming one. Her friend began to chatter on, something about the traffic, the perfection of the day, the wonder of it all. Rachel glanced out the tinted window at the intermittent rays of sunshine peeking through the buildings, glad that none of the conversation required her participation.

Her gaze was deflected by the prism of light shining through the new ring on her finger. The diamond wedding band Reid had given her sent a rainbow shower of sparkles across the interior of the limo as the sunlight filtered through it.

It was a beautiful, expensive symbol of something she hadn't given much thought to until now. This was legal. She folded her hand into a fist, an ineffective ploy to hide the obvious. She was now Mrs. Reid James. In name only or not, she was his wife. For better, for worse, until death—or one year—us do part.

The car stopped in front of his brownstone and everyone exited. Rachel knew they were supposed to host some sort of celebratory lunch. In a daze, she made her way up the steps, stumbling halfway up.

"Are you all right?" Reid asked as he took her arm.

"Yes," she said. "I'm fine."

He smiled at her, the now-familiar crinkles at the corners of his fabulous green eyes compelling her to turn the corners of her mouth upward in a reasonable facsimile.

They entered the cool foyer, Trudy's voice echoing in the hallway as she continued to chatter. Reality began to seep in as Rachel realized its source. Trudy was nervous. For her? Rachel wondered about that. Trudy had been all for this arrangement, so much so that she'd taken on the role of Reid's ally ever since her return from Ohio. She hadn't given Rachel time to *think*, let alone *re*think what she was doing.

But Rachel had to admit that everything had fallen into place. Even the dreaded conversation with her father had turned out better than she'd anticipated. She hadn't heard him sound so happy since the days before her mother's illness. He'd said he could tell that "something was up" between her and Reid the moment he'd set eyes on them standing together in front of the house.

So everyone was pleased. Everyone was in agreement. This was the sensible, right thing to do. Then why was her stomach in knots? Why was the prospect of sharing space with Reid James, even for a brief period of time, so terrifying to her?

She watched him walk down the hall, ushering his guests into the dining room with its black-lacquered Art Deco table set for lunch. The more she saw of him, the more she wondered about him. He had a style that, if she didn't know his background, she would have sworn must have been born as well as bred into him. He moved slowly, but purposefully, reminiscent of a not-too-hungry panther toying with his prey. There was an air of danger hidden under that veneer of polish and grace, a powerful masculinity that virtually oozed out of his pores, pulling her to him with an almost primal feminine response.

She felt a tremor run through her body, and to hide it, she reached up and pulled a spearlike, pearl-tipped pin out of her hat. Lifting the hat off her head, she dropped it on a chair and shook out her hair as Reid passed out long, elegant crystal flutes filled with champagne. She watched as he and Trudy engaged in their usual back-and-forth banter. Everyone was smiling. It seemed no one else reacted to him as she did.

Am I the only one who feels it?

Could that be why he made her hands shake, her knees knock, and her insides twist into a bittersweet knot every time his gaze locked with hers and he hit her with the intensity of those emerald eyes?

Like now.

Reid held out a glass and she declined, opting instead for mineral water.

"Good girl," he said with a smile, running a finger down the side of her cheek.

His touch was warm, dry, electric, and gone too fast. She leaned into it and almost lost her balance as he turned back to answer another of Trudy's barbs. The feeling of dread returned to Rachel in full force. What was this power he held over her? Was it only the obvious man-woman sexual attraction that she could no longer deny...or was there more to it? That was a question she did not wish to explore too thoroughly. It had taken her too long to gain her independence to ever give herself over to another person so completely.

But, sexual or not, the pull was there, no denying it. Her traitorous body responded to him in ways she couldn't define or control. Like the melting that came over her when she heard his voice, or the little blip in her stomach when he walked into the room. She didn't dare imagine how she would react if he ever *really* touched her.

Again.

And that was also part of the problem. Bits and pieces of their night together were returning to her with alarming frequency. She found herself blushing with this memory or that as it invaded her consciousness.

The things he'd done to her!

The things she'd done to him... She couldn't believe it had happened that way. But apparently it had, which in no small way explained Reid's confusion and enthusiasm for her. Which in no small way explained why she was so terrified.

After all, they'd never discussed exactly how "in name only" this marriage was to be. He'd had a life before her—a reputation that was well-known and as far as she knew, well-deserved. Did he intend to put those days behind him, or did he intend to continue his ladies' man life-style? And more importantly, where did she fit into all of this? What did he expect from her?

She both wildly dreaded and anticipated the outcome of that conversation. And it was a conversation she meant to have as soon as possible, and definitely before the sun went down.

Which meant *today*.

Reid held out the chair in the dining room for Rachel. She nodded almost absentmindedly as she slipped into the seat. With slow deliberation he moved to the other end and took his own seat at the head of the table.

He watched her all through lunch, an elegant affair of ice-cold, cracked crab salad and piping hot farfel pesto served with a perfectly chilled bottle of his best French champagne. She'd chosen the mineral water instead, which pleased him. She was taking care of herself and the child.

But she had been preoccupied all day, and he wondered what was on her mind. Even when they'd exchanged vows, she had been daydreaming and had to be prompted by Trudy with a polite poke in the back. While there was something charming and innocent about her distraction, it was also disturbing.

Was she having second thoughts? He hoped not. It was one of the reasons he'd asked Jules to come over earlier today. He had wanted to be sure that their marriage contract was in order and ready to be signed. He had promised her he'd put his words in writing, and he meant to honor that promise if only to reassure her that she could trust him.

He didn't know why it was so important to him, except that trust was something that had been in short supply in his own life, and he treated it like the rare commodity it was, holding it in the highest esteem. He also knew that she needed that trust to see her through this year. He recognized her reluctance to wed him for what it was: a deep-seated fear of having to depend on someone else.

He knew that fear. He'd lived with it seemingly forever, an aging dragon nipping at his heels with every encounter, every relationship, business or personal. Though he'd done neither in his life, he knew it would be harder for him to trust than to love. So in many ways he empathized with Rachel, and no matter how badly he wanted her and the child, he would do his damnedest to see that she was not hurt by any of this.

His reverie was broken as Trudy clinked the crystal goblet in front of her with her spoon. "Ladies and gentlemen, I propose a toast to the bride and groom." Jules and Charlotte lifted their glasses in salute as she continued. "To Reid and Rachel..." She smiled first at one, then the other, lowering her voice in an almost prayerlike whisper. "It was meant to be."

"Here, here," Jules said before downing the remainder of his champagne.

Charlotte daubed at her eyes with her white, linen napkin. "I'm so happy for you," she said to Reid, grasping his wrist in a firm, heartfelt grip. "This is just what you need."

Reid smiled at his colleague. "Ah," he said, "but are you ready for the aftermath?"

Charlotte and everyone else turned to him. "Aftermath?" she asked. "Of what?"

"Of today. When you return to the office, a letter awaits you. But I won't keep you in suspense. I'm taking a leave of absence. Indefinitely. It's all yours, Charlotte."

A nervous laugh from Jules diverted everyone's attention to him. "What exactly does that mean, Reid?" he asked.

"It means what it sounds like. I won't be running the operation for the time being."

"Exactly how long is that?" Jules continued.

"I haven't decided." Reid looked across the table to Rachel. "A year... or possibly more."

"But, Reid, you can't seriously think you can just walk away—"

"Ah, but, Jules, I can and I do. Charlotte can handle most of it. She has been, anyway, for longer than I can remember. Whatever she can't manage, my individual company's CEOs will deal with." Reid reached over and took hold of Charlotte's hand. "Close your mouth, Charlotte. And don't act surprised. We've talked about this many times."

"Yes . . . but I never thought you were serious."

"I'm serious."

"I don't understand," Jules said, his face a mask of confusion. "You never mentioned giving it up, Reid."

"I never had reason to." His gaze rested on Rachel. "Now I do."

He stared at Rachel, waiting for her to react to his announcement, but there was no visible change in her expression. What *was* she thinking? Suddenly, he wanted to shoo everyone away. He wanted to be alone with her, to reach out to her, to tell her everything was going to be all right. He would make it all right if it was the last thing he ever did in this life, for this mad, impulsive marriage was a gamble he knew in his heart he could not afford to lose.

"What are you going to do with yourself?" Jules asked, still uncomprehending, unwilling to let it go.

"Live."

Reid turned to Trudy who had uttered the one-word answer so succinctly and so pointedly correct. "Yes, Trudy, thank you." He turned to his attorney. "I'm going to live, Jules. I have enough money to do that, don't I?"

Jules's eyes widened. "You have enough money to do anything you want."

"So be it, then," Reid said, pushing his chair back. "If you'll all excuse us, Rachel and I have some things to discuss."

"But the papers—"

"In the den, Jules. Wait five minutes and meet us there." He walked to the other end of the long table and held out one hand as he pulled the chair out. "Shall we, Rachel?"

She was taken by surprise at his abrupt exit, hoping to have some time alone with Trudy before the day ended, but

Rachel complied, glancing at her friend over her shoulder as she followed him into the den.

"What's wrong?" she asked as he shut the sliding doors behind him and began to pace.

"I was about to ask you the same question," he said, pulling a toothpick from his suit-jacket pocket and placing it in his mouth.

He bit down on the minty piece of wood and almost vented an audible sigh of relief. He hadn't had a cigarette since that day in the motel room, determined to keep his promise to Rachel even if it killed him. He pulled the toothpick out of his mouth, turned it around and slipped it in once again, knowing how silly he must look, but not caring as the effort satisfied some primitive hand-to-mouth oral fixation he'd yet to cure even though his need for nicotine was virtually gone.

Rachel watched his act with interest. If she didn't know better, she'd say he was agitated. From what? Certainly not her.

"There's nothing wrong with me," she said.

"Then why have you been so distracted all day?"

Rachel shrugged and moved toward the window. "It's a big day for me," she said softly. "I don't get married every day."

"Nor do I."

She turned to him. Okay, she told herself. It was time. "What kind of marriage is this going to be? Exactly."

"Exactly the kind you wish it to be."

Rachel pressed her lips together. "It's *all* up to me? I find that hard to believe, Reid."

"Believe what you like. I will honor my promise to you."

"All promises? And vows, too?"

His eyes narrowed. "What are you getting at, Rachel?"

She hesitated. "You have a reputation, Reid."

"Greatly exaggerated, Rachel."

"That may be so, but I'd like to make one thing clear. I won't be humiliated."

"Are you asking if there will be other women?"

"Yes."

He smiled slowly, but didn't answer right away. She wondered what was going through his mind. "There will be no other women, Rachel."

She hadn't expected such quick agreement. She lifted her eyebrows in surprise. "Do you mean you won't . . . I mean, you intend to remain—"

"Remain celibate? If that's what you wish."

"I *wish* you'd stop saying that and answer me."

Reid pulled the mangled toothpick out of his mouth and dropped it into an ashtray. With slow deliberation, he walked over to where Rachel was standing and faced her. He was so close, she could feel his body heat emanate out to her. His scent filled her nostrils with each breath she took, and her insides twisted in response. He pinned her with his eyes and, as usual, she couldn't look away, so she just stood there, waiting.

She didn't know what to do with her hands, wanting to insinuate them inside the lapels of his suit jacket and rub her palms against his chest. But she couldn't do that, so she just left them dangling at her sides, feeling awkward and unnecessary.

"I think we need to get some things straight," he said. Then, lifting one of her useless hands, he kissed the palm and placed it on his shoulder, before repeating the action with the other.

Rachel swallowed. "Such as?"

He rested his hands firmly at her waist, pulling her closer. "What do you want me to say, Rachel? That I want this to be a real marriage? One where we not only live together, but share the same bed?" His eyes scanned her face, they moved lower to her neck, her chest. "Do you want to hear that I desire you, want to make love with you again?" He reached up and unbuttoned the top, then the second button of her suit, exposing her lacy beige bra to his gaze. "Do you want to hear those words from me? Do you want me to ask you to be my wife in every way, to try it out, to see if we can make something more out of this?" He ran the backs of his knuckles across the tips of her breasts. Instantly, her nipples hardened. He smiled at her response and leaned his head forward, his breath grazing her ear as he whispered, "Then, please, Rachel, consider yourself asked."

Before she could say a word, he pulled her up against him and brushed his mouth against hers. Her eyes fluttered closed at the contact.

"Oh, yes, Rachel, consider yourself *very* asked." With care, he baby-kissed her top lip, then her bottom, then separated her lips with the pad of his thumb.

"Open," he said, and a deluge of memories of the first time he'd said that word to her swirled into her head. She ran her hands down from his shoulders to his chest, scrunching the material of his jacket in her fists as she obeyed his command.

When his tongue touched hers, Rachel leaned into the kiss. He plundered the inside of her mouth with deep, erotic strokes of his tongue, tasting, drinking, taking all she had to give.

Rachel was weak with desire, lost in a misty world only he seemed able to create for her. Visions of past times he'd kissed her like this danced in her head as his hands caressed her back, roamed lower to her waist, and finally found and cupped her bottom, kneading the soft flesh as he pressed her fully against him.

Her insides turned to warm, melting cream as her hips cradled his hard arousal. She wanted him. Lord, she couldn't remember ever wanting anything as badly as she wanted him right now. The memories had come back, yes, but the reality was oh, so much better. He reached up under her jacket. His hands instinctively knew how to touch her in ways she didn't even know would turn her on. How could that be? she wondered as she attempted to get closer to him, to rub herself into him, to wrap herself around him.

Reid broke free and stepped back so abruptly she almost lost her balance. He was breathing heavily, his body stiff, still, tight. His nostrils flared as he sucked in air.

For the longest moment they stared at each other. Rachel's lips tingled with the aftermath of his kisses, her body throbbed from his touch, her mind craved more. She lifted her fingertips to her swollen lips as if in silent tribute.

Reid took a step forward, reached out and rebuttoned her jacket quickly, efficiently. "Have I answered all your questions?" he asked.

Rachel tried to say something, but no words emerged. She was as equally stunned by his revelation as she was by his kiss—stunned, elated, horrified, and so heart-poundingly excited that if he made another move toward her, she'd fall into his arms on a sigh and a breathy "yes." A discreet knock interrupted them, but Reid ignored it. "Well, Rachel? Have I?"

"Yes," she managed to respond.

"And . . . your answer?"

She shook her head and turned away from him. "I don't know . . ."

Rachel knew what she wanted to say, knew that deep down in her heart she wanted the same things he said he wanted. Nothing would please her more than to try to make this marriage work, to try to make it a "real" marriage, as he'd asked. Thoughts swirled through her head—of sharing a bed with him, being naked in his arms, waking in the morning with his hand cradling her stomach as it grew bigger with their child—and they made her so weak with want and longing that she could barely muster enough energy to breathe.

Yet something stopped her.

She still harbored some unnamed, unexplainable, deep-down fear that this wasn't quite real, that it was all a joke, that he was toying with her, playing a game to get what he wanted: the baby.

After all, why would someone like him, who could have anyone, want her like this? Not that she didn't think herself worthy, but he'd had his choice of all the women in the world. There was only one thing that made her special, made her different, made her stand out, and that was the baby—his baby.

And she couldn't dissuade herself that the baby had to be the reason he wanted her at all in his life.

She couldn't do it. She couldn't put herself in that position, to open herself up to fall in love with him so irrevocably—as she now understood she could very easily do—that she would lose her very soul. She'd been hurt too much by people who were supposed to love her. It was too soon and too hard to leave herself open to that hurt again.

She felt him walk up behind her. He turned her around. Lifting her chin, he forced her to look up at him. For the longest moment, he scanned her face, looking for what she wasn't sure.

Rachel wanted so much to reach up to him, touch his face, tell him she wanted those same things—

The knock sounded again, louder this time. She clenched her fists and pulled away from him. "You'd better answer that."

Reid stared at her back, feeling his blood pound through his veins at her rejection. His jaw tightened with the frustration and humiliation he felt at laying his feelings on the line to her.

But he wasn't about to give up.

He took a deep, cleansing breath and blew it out. Okay, he'd taken a chance and lost. It wasn't the first time he'd acted the fool and it wouldn't be the last. This was as new to her as it was to him. If it was time she needed, he would see that she got it.

The knock was more emphatic.

"Yes?" Reid called out just as emphatically.

Jules slid open one half of the door and poked his head through. "Are you ready for me?"

"Come in, Jules," Reid said.

Rachel nodded as Jules greeted her. She watched as he took a seat on the white leather sofa and placed his cherry leather briefcase on top of the glass coffee table. Snapping open the locks, he took out several folders and spread them in front of him. Then he picked one and held it out to Rachel.

"For me?"

"Yes," Jules said, glancing back and forth from Reid to Rachel. "Hasn't Reid explained?"

"No," she said. "What—"

"Read it," Reid said.

She glanced at him sharply. "May I sit?"

"Please do."

Not quite recovered from his touch, his kiss, or his offer, Rachel folded her skirt beneath her with one hand as she sat with all the dignity she could muster on the edge of the club chair. As she opened the folder, she felt her stomach drop as the words in bold print jumped out at her: Morgan/James Nuptial Agreement.

She looked up at Reid. "This is..."

"My words to you. In writing. As promised." Their gazes locked. "I suggest you read it," he said more softly than before.

She did. With slow deliberation, she read a page at a time, the legalese blurring after the fifth page, but the message getting through loud and clear.

"Why are you doing this?" she asked.

"I thought it was what you wanted," he answered, a sincere, puzzled expression on his face.

"I wanted your word."

"And now you have it."

"Your word, Reid—" she shook the papers in the air "—not some contract!"

"The contract is your protection, Rachel."

"Have you read it?" she asked.

"I know what it says."

"Do you? And what is that?"

"Essentially, it states that after one year, you are free to go, move on, or whatever you wish. A mutually agreed-upon settlement will be negotiated for you and the child."

"And that's that?" she asked, her heart fluttering in her chest. "But you just said—"

"Rachel, you must understand," Jules interjected. "Reid is a very wealthy man. A divorce will put him in a very precarious position. The agreement must protect both of you."

"It makes me sound like a gold digger, a fortune hunter." How could he hand this to her after what he'd just said? She felt the bile rise to her throat. "I give you my word that when this year is up I won't go after any of your money, Reid. That will have to be good enough." She stood and dropped the folder onto the coffee table. "I told you this wasn't about money. I'm not for sale. And I'm not signing that."

"You must—"

"Be quiet, Jules."

"But, Reid, listen to me. As your ex-wife she'll be entitled to half of everything you have."

Reid turned to Jules. His face was stone cold, implacable, his eyes a wintry green. "If she takes half of my money, Jules, how much will I have left?" he asked conversationally.

"Well...I don't know exactly. That would have to be determined by—"

"Will I be poor?"

"Poor? Lord, Reid, of course not!"

"Then it's not something I need worry about, is it?" He turned to Rachel. "Leave us alone, will you, Jules?"

"Reid, I must protest. As your attorney, it's my duty to advise you—"

His eyes never leaving Rachel's, he added, "Go, Jules. Now."

Rachel heard the shuffle of papers. Her peripheral vision even caught a piece of Jules as he left the room. She heard the sound of the sliding doors behind him. And then the quiet. They were alone.

His eyes held hers and she watched the cold, clear green turn to fiery emerald. He held out his hand, but she didn't take it. "Everything you said before was just for show, wasn't it, Reid?" she asked.

"I meant every word I said, Rachel."

"Then why this contract?"

"I thought you wanted it."

She shook her head. "No. No, I don't."

Reid picked the folder up from the table and walked over to the other side of the room. He dropped it into the white marble trash container. "Consider it gone."

Rachel felt herself relax with his action. She didn't know why she'd reacted that way to the contract, but it had made her feel cheap, bought, paid for. It made her feel as if she were here only to make a baby for him, and then she would be on her way. It made her feel sick.

She wanted more from him. So much more. She felt tears threatening, and bit her lip to stave them off. Was she so wrong to want to be wanted for herself?

"I didn't mean to cause Jules a problem," she said as Reid returned to her side.

"Don't worry about Jules."

"I don't really know what I'm doing here, Reid. This has all happened so fast." She looked up at him, feeling the tears pool behind her eyes. "I'm scared."

"Don't you think I am, too?"

"You?"

"Yes, me. This is a whole new experience for me, as well."

"Were you serious about taking a leave of absence from work?"

"Quite."

"What will you do?"

"Exactly what Trudy suggested. Live." He put out his hand. "*Live* with me, Rachel." Tentatively she placed her hand into his palm. His fingers closed around her hand, and she looked up at him. "Trust, Rachel. If this isn't about money, then it must be about trust. We're both taking a chance, maybe a bigger one than we've ever taken in our lives. I'm ready to give it a try."

"Trust," she said. "I trust you, Reid. I don't know why exactly, but I do."

"Then that's a first step."

She was just about to ask him what the second step could possibly be when Trudy called out to them from the partially closed doors. "Mind if I come in? Charlotte and I have to get back to the office. We just wanted to say goodbye."

Reid waved them in. Charlotte walked to him and began asking work-related questions as Trudy made a beeline toward Rachel.

As they hugged goodbye, Trudy whispered in her ear, "Are you going to sleep with him tonight?"

"Trudy!" Rachel stage whispered.

"Well, are you?"

"I—don't... No, of course not."

"Has he asked?"

"Well, yes... he has, in a manner of speaking, but—"

"Don't you want to?"

"Trudy, please. I haven't even thought about it," Rachel lied, glancing over at Charlotte and Reid to be sure they were still engrossed in their business discussion.

"I don't believe that."

"It's true."

"Then you're crazier than I thought. There are a million women out there in this city alone who would kill to trade places with you right now, girl."

"Maybe so, but it's me who has to make the decision."

"You may enjoy it, Rachel."

She gave her friend a wry grin. "That's what I'm afraid of."

"Ready?" Charlotte called to Trudy.

"Coming," Trudy replied. She gave Rachel another quick hug. "Call me," she said. "Tomorrow morning." She looked Rachel in the eye as she held her shoulder-length away. "First thing."

Charlotte came over and kissed Rachel's cheek. "Be patient with him," she whispered. "He's a wonderful man, much more wonderful than even he knows."

Rachel returned a hug. She genuinely liked Charlotte and was learning to trust her almost as much as Reid did. "I'll try," she said.

Trudy air-kissed Reid as she made her way toward the door. He held it for her as Charlotte and Rachel said their goodbyes.

"Take care of her, Reid," Trudy said.

"I plan to," he answered.

"You know," Trudy said with a hand on her hip. "If you'd use a little of that famous charm of yours on Rachel, you may be surprised at what you get."

"Such as?"

"She could fall in love with you."

He laughed. "Highly unlikely."

"You could fall in love with her."

He stopped laughing. "Go back to work, Trudy."

She grinned, then chuckled. "This could be fun," she said, saluted, then exited with Charlotte close behind.

Reid shut the door and stood with his back to Rachel for a long moment. When he turned, he had the most peculiar look on his face. Rachel felt as if he were examining her under a microscope.

"What is it?" she asked.

He shook his head, more to himself than to her. "Nothing," he answered, Trudy's words still ringing in his ears.

Falling in love. Ridiculous! Trudy was insane. This wasn't any more about love than it was about money, and he was sure that Rachel felt the same way. Trust, companionship, common interests, raising the child together—these were the important things. Love was not necessary. That type of unstable emotion would only confuse things. It was a non-issue. He'd never had any need for it, and he'd done just fine.

He wasn't even sure it existed.

He looked up at Rachel. She was staring at him as if he had two heads. Maybe he did.

"I'd like to freshen up," Rachel said, hoping that a little distance would dissipate this new awkwardness.

"Certainly," he said. "Your bags are upstairs." He motioned toward the spiral staircase with his hand, and Rachel led the way up to the next level.

And then, suddenly, unexpectedly, with no preparation whatsoever, she was there. Back in his bedroom. The white room from her dream.

Everything was still, and bright, unlike the last time she'd been here. The air conditioner was humming as the sunlight filtered through the white voile curtains. The king-size brass bed had its white netting gathered to the ceiling. It dominated the room. Her bags were at the foot of the bed symmetrically standing at attention according to size. Her smaller, overnight bag lay unzipped on top of the white satin comforter.

"I thought we'd spend the night here, and make the trip to Connecticut tomorrow."

Panic forced her throat closed. She couldn't spend the night here, not in this room, and certainly not in this bed!

Without thinking, she turned to him. "I can't."

"What?"

"I can't stay here."

"Why not?"

"This room—I can't, that's all."

Reid's eyes narrowed. "Remembering, Rachel?"

"Some."

"Was it so awful you can't stand being here again?" He couldn't believe how bothered he was by her obvious revulsion to his room . . . his bed.

She shook her head. "No, of course not."

"Then why—"

"It's hot."

"I'll turn the air up."

"It's all *white*," she said.

"You hate white?"

How could she explain about the dream without sounding like an idiot? "I'd just rather not stay here. That's all."

Patience, he said to himself. "Okay." He nodded slowly several times. "Okay. We'll leave this afternoon for

Connecticut. It's cooler up there. There are three bedrooms. Not a white one in the bunch. You may have your pick."

Rachel knew he was annoyed, but she couldn't help herself. There was no way on earth she could bring herself to sleep in this bed tonight. "I'd like that."

He shook his head. "Fine. I'll wait for you downstairs." He stopped at the door. "Rachel?"

She turned to him. "Yes?"

"I know we never came to any conclusions, but whether we live together as man and wife, I do want to make it perfectly clear that I want this marriage to be legal."

"I thought it was legal."

"Legal in every way."

Rachel brought her hand up to her neck, a reaction to her fluttering pulse in her neck. "Can you be more specific?" she asked, trying her best to sound as matter-of-fact as he.

"Yes. Connecticut or here, I want us to consummate the marriage."

Consummate. The word hung in the air between them. Such an old-fashioned word, she thought, that did, indeed, say it all. His use of it said a lot about him, too. It added to that old-worldliness that clung to him like an outer garment, a formalness that made him seem as if he were from another time, another place, raised in a different age with a different set of rules.

"I see..." She swallowed. "When... do you propose we should..."

"Soon. That is, if you are able."

He was giving her an out. She could, of course, pretend she didn't feel well, blame it on the pregnancy, and drag it out for who knew how long. His concern for her and the baby would be too great for him to push. She knew that, but somehow couldn't bring herself to lie.

Reid's eyes met hers. She saw many things there. Determination—without a doubt—but so much more, not the least of which was an uncertainty that suddenly endeared him to her. A fine layer of perspiration bathed the back of her neck. "How soon?"

Reid felt his stomach twist as a piercing arrow of white-hot desire zapped through him. He'd taken a chance with his request and had come out on top. The image made his head swim. He pinned her with his eyes, held her captive. "I don't see any reason in putting it off, do you?"

"No," she said a bit too quickly. "No reason. Whenever you say."

On a wing and a prayer, he uttered the final challenge. "Tonight, then."

Rachel nodded slowly. "That will be fine."

Tonight.

Six

It was nothing like she'd imagined. She'd thought grand, elegant, a sprawling version of his town house with trees. It was anything but.

It was beautiful.

Set at least half a mile off the road, the house had all the rustic charm of an advertisement for country retreats. It had no airs about it, no artifice of any kind. Sturdy, naturally stained oak gave it an ordinary touch she did not associate with someone like Reid. Or at least the Reid that she—and everyone else—thought they knew.

If the New York town house was the urbane, polished Reid James, then the Connecticut country house represented his alter ego, a down-to-basics side of him he'd never shown to anyone.

This was a home, quaint, understated, hospitable. As Rachel exited from the car, the wraparound porch seemed to reach out to her like giant arms extended in welcome.

Rachel felt the excitement build in her. She stood behind Reid as he fumbled with the old lock. She was thrilled to be here, excited to view what lay behind the door. Her face lit up with a beaming smile of anticipation.

Then the door swung inward on a loud creak and Reid turned to her. The look on his face stopped her cold. It was dead serious, and a feeling of imminent dread washed over her. Her smiled faded. "What is it?" she asked.

"Let's do this right," he answered, and, before she could say another word, he scooped her up into his arms and carried her over the threshold.

Rachel held on to his neck tightly. He didn't put her down right away, but swung her around as he surveyed the interior.

"I haven't been here in ages," he said apologetically as he readjusted her weight in his arms. "It's very simple, kind of small, and underdecorated."

"'Underdecorated'?" she repeated breathlessly. Her heart was pounding as much from trying to fathom his mercurial moods as from being swept off her feet.

Reid gazed into her eyes. They were clear, gray, and wide with wonder. He hadn't realized until he'd put the key in the lock how badly he'd wanted her to like this place. From the look on her face, she was in shock. She'd probably been expecting a mansion on a waterfront estate. He felt the need to compensate for the poor showing.

Without thinking, he leaned down and brushed his lips against hers. She responded by parting her lips, and he lost no time in deepening the kiss. A wave of longing gripped him as her tongue touched his, but he knew he had to let her go...and now, before he lost control, before he laid her down right here in the hallway and made love to her. The day had been endless, the drive up tense. He was too tightly wound to give in to this kiss, and too afraid of what would happen if he did.

This wasn't the way he wanted it to be. If they were to make love tonight, it had to be special, so perfect that she would remember it forever...and so satisfying that she would want him again....and again.

He lifted his lips from hers. "For luck," he said with a smile, trying to lighten the mood and dispel her obvious confusion. He tightened his hold on her for an instant before slowly releasing her, allowing her body to slide against his as he set her onto her feet.

Reid took an awkward step back, running a hand through his hair to cover the emotion he was feeling. It ran hard and deep, and took him by surprise. The sight of her standing here in this house, this home, this one place on earth that had spoken to him, that had said it was somewhere that he belonged, shook him up more than he could have imagined.

He turned from her, hoping to hide the raw emotion that must show on his face. With a wave of his hand, he indicated the living room. "It needs a lot of work. You can fix it up any way you want," he said.

Rachel stepped up beside him as her gaze swept the first floor. "From what I can see, it's perfect."

Reid cupped her face in his hand as the thought flitted through his mind. *As are you.* And then he did smile. "Come on. I'll show you around."

He held out his hand, and she took it, leading her into the living room.

It wasn't big, but very cozy. A fireplace stood in the center of the far wall with a lounge chair and two couches facing each other in front of it. An oak chair rail ran around the diameter with four-by-eight oak beams crisscrossing the ceiling. The furniture was Early American and a bit faded, but with a lot of life left in it and very usable.

Rachel's mind started racing as Reid led her through the rest of the first floor and into the kitchen/dining area that overlooked a backyard that was overgrown and in need of some tender loving care.

Reid ran a hand through some spiderwebs that hung across the bay window. "The place hasn't been used much, as you can see."

She sat on one of the wooden chairs and stretched her legs out in front of her. "I must admit, I'm surprised."

"And disappointed," he said.

"No! Not at all. Quite the contrary. I love the place. But I was expecting something very grand. Like the town house."

"Yeah. Well, I think that's one of the reasons I bought it."

"And what were the other reasons?"

Reid walked around her and sat on the window seat. He didn't answer. His body was turned from her, staring out at the overgrown yard, but his stiff posture spoke volumes. He sat straight and still for a very long time.

The room was quiet, the last of the day's light fading. Rachel folded her hands in her lap, prepared to wait for him to speak. She sensed he'd gone off somewhere, to another time, another place. She held her breath in hopes that he would share those thoughts with her, that she would get an opportunity to know him better, to gain some insight into what made Reid James tick.

He didn't disappoint her.

"Do you really want to know?" he asked over his shoulder.

"Yes, I do."

He smiled, a sad half grin that made her heart skip a beat.

"When I was a kid growing up in the orphanage, I used to dream about a place like this. A home in the country. Nothing big or special, but an ordinary place with a yard to run around in and a room with a fireplace where the family would gather at Christmas and decorate the tree..."

"Reid, you don't have to—"

"It's all right, Rachel. I'm not getting maudlin on you. And I'm not complaining. Lots of people have had it much, much worse than me."

Rachel thought of her own childhood, her mother's gentle guiding hand, the special way she made her feel as a little girl. How horrible it must have been for him to have never even met either of his parents. Her throat tightened with emotion and she put a hand to her abdomen, a protective gesture and a pledge to the life she carried within.

She rose and walked up behind him. Tentatively, she put a hand on his shoulder. "You must have been very lonely."

He stood abruptly, shrugged his shoulders, and her hand dropped away. "No more than other kids in less than ideal situations, I suppose. Come on, let's finish the tour. You'll want to start thinking of ideas to fix the place up."

Rachel touched his arm. "I don't want to change a thing." Their eyes met. "I love it."

Reid measured her sincerity for a moment. "You haven't seen upstairs yet."

"I don't have to. It's better than I ever imagined."

"Really?"

"Yes."

He grinned at her, not believing how pleased he was that she liked the house as is. He'd felt exactly the same way when he'd bought it on a whim five years ago. He'd been driving through the countryside returning from a less-than-memorable trip with an equally forgettable blonde when he'd seen the For Sale sign.

A bell had gone off in his head. He'd stopped and knocked on the door. An elderly woman had answered. She'd been widowed and wanted to sell and move to a warmer climate. He'd written her a check on the spot, yet, as if he'd been waiting for a reason to return, he'd been back no more than twice over the years.

This marriage aside, buying this old house had been one of the more impulsive things he'd done in his life. Though he'd never taken the time to analyze it, somewhere in his subconscious mind, owning it provided a secret sense of security that in his more rational times he'd argue the need for.

He took her hand. "Let's check out the upstairs."

Rachel let him lead the way to the second-floor landing. She peered through the open stairway as she ascended. Feeling like a little girl in a playhouse, she pulled herself along the railing that ran the length of the hallway, the only protection between the floors.

Reid stopped, and she bumped into his back. "The first bedroom," he said, swinging the door inward. He took a step back to allow her first entrance. "And you will notice, no white."

Rachel's look chided him over her shoulder. "No. No white."

Two twin beds separated by a pine nightstand, plain, simple, functional. The second room was smaller, with only a twin bed and dresser, and Rachel's mind registered that this would be a perfect size for a nursery. At the end of the hallway were two steps, a right-turn landing and two more steps leading up to the third bedroom.

Rachel's eyes filled with joy at the sight of it. It wasn't that it was a big room, or even a particularly pretty room. Yet the way the waning light filtered through the shades created an almost ethereal golden glow over the room. It reminded her of a Biblical setting just standing in wait for an angel to appear.

There was a cherrywood armoire, vanity dresser, two small night tables on either side of a full-size bed, and in the corner, a small, round, table skirted to match the patchwork bedspread and curtains.

Rachel smiled as she ran her hand over the material. Someone had taken loving care with every stitch.

Reid stepped beside her. "You like it?"

She nodded.

"It's yours."

He hadn't said "ours," but "yours."

She wondered what that meant, but said only, "Thank you."

"Well, you've seen the house. How about some dinner? Are you hungry?"

The minute the words left his mouth, Rachel was hit with an unreasonable craving for fried rice. Ever since Trudy had brought the Chinese food home to her the day she'd gone to the doctor, she'd developed this almost hysterical need for the dish at odd times of the day and night. "I'm starving."

"We could go out." She made a face. "Okay...how about take-out?"

"Chinese?"

He laughed. "If that's what you want."

"I'd do anything for some fried rice right now."

"That's a hell of an offer, Rachel."

She laughed. "Lo mein, too."

Reid couldn't have been more accommodating. He unpacked the car, refusing even the slightest help from her, then he left to find a Chinese take-out restaurant in the wilds of Connecticut. Which turned out to be no easy feat, as he was gone for more than an hour.

"Lo mein, fried rice, beef with broccoli, butterfly shrimp, chicken with pea pods—"

"Whoa! How much did you get?"

"I forgot to ask you what you wanted as a main course. I ordered one from each category."

He ate with chopsticks, she shoveled food into her mouth with a soupspoon. "How do you *do* that?" she asked between mouthfuls.

"I did a lot of business in Hong Kong several years ago and learned. Here—" he held out a shrimp to her "—try it."

"I don't think—"

"Come on, Rachel. Give it a try. Open . . ."

Reid dangled the food above her lips as if he were distributing a sacrament. Rachel had to lift her head and open wide to receive the morsel. He dipped the shrimp into her mouth. As her lips closed around it, he slowly slid the chopsticks out, the coarse wood grazing against the tender insides of her lips.

Their eyes met. Rachel held the food in her mouth for a long moment before she began to chew. His gaze followed her movements, watching until she had swallowed.

"It's easy," he said softly, "once you get the hang of it."

"I don't think I could. I'm not very good with my hands."

A half smile creased his face. "Oh, I wouldn't say that. Like anything else, it takes practice. The better you become, the more you'll enjoy it."

Somehow Rachel felt they weren't exactly talking about chopsticks anymore. She felt the heat rise to her face and she bent her head, paying an inordinate amount of attention to the food remaining on her plate.

"Tea?"

Rachel looked up. Reid held a teapot aloft.

"Yes, please," she said, pushing her mug forward.

Reid filled it to the top with the steaming liquid. He nudged the mug toward her before refilling his own. Rachel lifted the mug and sipped. She shut her eyes as the tea's warmth spread through her.

"You're tired," he said.

"A little."

"A lot. Why don't you take that with you and go on up to bed? I'll clean up."

Rachel looked at him. What was he suggesting? Was he asking her to "get ready" for the night? Was he going to join her?

"Okay," she answered, rising from the table with the mug in her hand.

"Good night, Rachel."

"Aren't you . . . coming, too?"

"No. Not right now. I have some things to do around here."

"Well, then, I'll say good-night."

Rachel held up the nightgown for inspection. The thin, white satin glistened in the light of the fire Reid had set once the sun went down and the cool evening air brought a chill into the house. Absentmindedly, she ran her hand over the shiny pattern. Of course, she wasn't really going to *wear* it.

Trudy had bought it for her. "Your trousseau," she'd said, and Rachel had been too polite to refuse the gift. She really had no plans to ever put it on. She had been sure she'd never have *occasion* to wear it.

But now she had.

He'd asked.

She'd agreed.

Tonight was the night.

A chill ran down the middle of her back despite the fact that the room was as warm as toast. Reid hadn't followed her upstairs, and though Rachel appreciated the solitude, she was still ambivalent about what the balance of this night held in store for her.

Soon after she'd climbed the stairs to the master bedroom, the tension of the day had hit her squarely between the eyes. She felt beyond tired all the way to weary. A long soak in the claw-foot tub had done wonders to drain away the stress, but did little to still her fears about the coming night.

She wanted to make love with him. She wanted it more than she could ever remember wanting anything.

But she was scared.

The woman he remembered from that summer night at his town house was not someone she knew. That woman was a figment of his imagination—and perhaps hers, as well. That woman had been carefree, uninhibited, a natural lover, open and willing to explore all he had to offer.

Perhaps somewhere deep inside that passionate woman existed, but Rachel couldn't conjure her up at will. Even with her limited sexual experience, she knew she wasn't the best lover. What would Reid expect from the real her?

Rachel dropped the nightgown on the bed and buried her face in her hands. She was sure the real her would disappoint him terribly. And she didn't want to do that, not tonight, especially if this was to be the only night they would ever make love again.

The thought pierced her heart. Everything was too uncertain, too temporary, for her to take any joy in this. She wanted him, needed him, but there was a time limit to what she could expect from him. And she couldn't complain. He'd let her set all the rules, and he had meticulously followed her wishes. So the birth of the baby was a two-sided coin—she wanted the child more than life itself, yet she dreaded the inevitable outcome once it was born.

The old-fashioned wind-up alarm clock on the nightstand ticked loudly. It was late, and still he hadn't appeared. Was he coming to her? Or would he stay away tonight? This mental debate was silly, she thought. Why not just march right on downstairs and ask his intentions?

But she couldn't bring herself to do that. It would seem as if she was asking him to make love with her. And what was wrong with that? she asked herself. Was it so wrong for her to take the initiative? She should just don this beautiful nightgown and walk into the kitchen and ask him.

"Excuse me, Reid," she said out loud to the empty room. "Are we going to *consummate* this marriage tonight or not?"

The thought of it made her giggle. Who was she kidding? Never in a million years would she have the nerve to do something like that. He'd fall down dead if she ever asked him point-blank.

And it would certainly serve him right, leaving her hanging here, not knowing if she should dress, or *undress,* lie on the bed seductively arranged, or snuggle under the covers for the night.

She decided to do both. Stripping out of her robe, she wiggled into the nightgown, running her hands over the silky material as it glided down her body into place. She examined herself in the mirror, both pleased and daunted by what she saw.

Her breasts were so full, they strained against the material, bulging from the sides and top of the heart-shaped neckline. Despite the fact that she knew it was more the nightgown's doing than her body's, she *did* look seductive.

She crossed her arms across her chest as she wondered if that was good or bad.

Turning off the lamp, Rachel used the step stool to climb up onto the high bed. She slid under the quilt and pulled it up to her chest, tucking it so that she was what she hoped was sufficiently covered. The warmth of the fire coupled with her exhaustion left her little time to ruminate about her fate. She shut her eyes, and in minutes, was asleep.

Her heart was pounding as she awoke with a start, from what, at first, she wasn't sure. And then she knew. Reid stood framed in the doorway, his features hidden by the flickering light of the fire. Rachel had no idea what time it was as the clock was turned from her view. She knew she had slept, but for how long, she couldn't tell. She wondered if he knew she'd awakened, then jumped when she heard him speak.

"Tell me it's okay for me to be here."

With a shaky arm, Rachel pushed herself up. "It's okay for you to be here."

Reid didn't approach the bed, didn't shut the door behind him, but then, there was no need. They were alone in the house. He walked over to the fireplace and placed another log on the few remaining burning embers. He was chewing on one of those toothpicks, she noticed, a sure sign that he was either agitated or deep in thought.

"What time is it?" she asked softly.

"Almost dawn. I couldn't sleep," he said, his back to her as he rested a hand on the rough wooden mantel. "Do you want me to go?" he asked as he looked at her over his shoulder.

She knew he sensed her apprehension, but Rachel shook her head firmly. "No."

He threw the toothpick into the fire and walked over to the edge of the bed. Rachel pushed her tousled hair away from her face, and as she did, the quilt fell to her waist. Reid's gaze was drawn to the straining neckline of her nightgown. He reached for the hem of the quilt and, with a flick of his wrist, peeled it down from her body and flipped it away to the bottom of the bed.

"I like it," he said, his eyes taking in every inch of the white satin nightgown.

"Trudy bought it for me."

"Remind me to give her a raise."

Rachel's laugh was strangled by her nerves. He was still dressed in his shirt and jeans. She wondered what he had been doing all this time while she'd slept. She wondered more what he was doing here. Now. At almost dawn. Her pulse throbbed in her throat, and she could hear the dull beat of her heart in her ears.

With a prayer and a dare to herself, Rachel scooted over to make room for him in the bed. Without a word, she patted the space beside her. She ignored the tingling sensation at the back of her neck as Reid sat, leaning his weight on one hand as he kept a slight distance.

"Do you have any idea how much I want you, Rachel?" he asked, so softly, so simply, she felt herself melt with the admission.

"No, tell me."

"I'd rather show you."

She reached up and caressed the side of his face. "Then do it, Reid. Please do."

She strained forward to meet him halfway as his mouth reached out to hers. She parted her lips for him, the way she knew he liked it, the way that gave him total access to her, the way she craved. The heat and the hunger surprised her, though why that should be, she couldn't fathom. Each time he kissed her was the same. It made her weak with longing to be taken by him, as possessed in body as she was already in soul.

His arms came around her and she molded herself to him. What was it about him that made her turn to jelly? Did he affect other women this way, or only her? Like his expertise with the chopsticks, he was practiced, he was smooth, he knew exactly what he was doing. Unlike her, who was only able to follow his lead.

"Relax," he whispered in her hair as he planted small kisses around her neck and behind her ear.

"I can't."

He pulled at the thin straps of her nightgown and it fell from her shoulders. With his fingertips, he grazed the soft, full tops of her almost-exposed breasts.

"Tell me you don't want this and I'll leave."

"No. Don't go."

He pushed aside the remaining fabric, baring her to the waist. When he cupped her breast fully in his hand, she jumped back from him.

"Ah, sweetheart, you're driving me crazy." Reid pulled back.

"No. Please. Stay."

"Rachel, make up your mind. What do you want me to do?"

"Stay," she said. "Definitely stay. Just..."

"Just what?"

"Well, maybe it would be better if you took your clothes off."

"All of them?"

She swallowed. "Yes."

Reid got up off the bed and started to unbutton his shirt, pull his shirttails out of his jeans and kick off his shoes, a might too quickly, she viewed, as if he was afraid she'd change her mind. Which she might.

Bravely, without adjusting her nightgown, Rachel pushed herself up onto her knees and shimmied to the edge of the bed just as the shirt slipped from his shoulders. She stopped cold in front of him, her hands reaching out but not touching his chest.

Reid rolled the shirt up into a ball and threw it somewhere across the room. "How about some help?" he asked softly. There was only one thing left on him. When she didn't move, he reached between them and unsnapped his jeans, but that was all. He didn't unzip them, offering himself to her instead. "Go ahead, Rachel. Do it."

Rachel shut her eyes. Leaning forward she rested her cheek against his chest, her bare breasts grazing the taut muscles of his abdomen. She rubbed herself against him like a loving cat. A faint mixture of man and cologne filled her nostrils as her hands reached up and slowly, but very purposely, unzipped his jeans. She felt the sound of his heart thumping in his chest and it made her bold enough to hook her thumbs into the waistband and pull down.

She felt, then saw, that he was wearing short silk boxers, the color of which she couldn't tell. As the jeans caught somewhere in the vicinity of his ankles, she ran her hands over his sides and around to his hard buttocks. The feel of his skin through the slick softness of the material made her shake inside.

Rachel kissed his chest as her hands massaged him, roaming ever bolder as she reached around front to the source of his desire. His quick intake of breath told her an instant before she touched him that he would already be aroused—hard, hot and ready to wreak havoc with her senses.

"Rachel..."

It was more than her name, it was an entreaty, a moan from the deep recesses of his soul, and she delighted in its sound. She caressed every inch of him with both hands—the length of him, the width of him, over, under, and around him, through the filmy material until she felt his heat would consume her.

She never knew that touching a man like this, making him crazy with want, could be so exciting, so arousing for herself, so satisfying, so needful. She rested back on her knees and lowered her face to him, moistening the silk fabric with her breath as she nuzzled his erection.

It was at once all too much and not enough for Reid. He grabbed her by the arms and lifted her lips to his. Without pause, his tongue swept into her mouth, a kiss so deep with need and longing that it made them both shake with want and wonder.

He released her and she fell back onto the bed. Within seconds, he shrugged out of the remainder of his clothing, and was gloriously naked beside her. He kissed her sensitive breasts with feather-light kisses before gently suckling first one side, then the other until her nipples were swollen and distended.

"Rachel..." He chanted her name again and again as he fanned her breasts with his warm breath.

Rachel shifted, turning her body toward him, running her smooth leg against his hair-roughened one. Reid reached down and cupped her through the satin gown. He instantly felt the dampness seep through onto his hand.

Reid shut his eyes, in awe at her ability to always surprise him, to always thrill him. The sweet, wonderful, shy Rachel was in reality all of those things and none of them. She was a woman he'd dreamed of having in his life, in his bed, and the dream-come-to-life was almost too much for him to believe.

Rachel was embarrassed by the wetness he encountered. She tried to clamp her legs together, but it was too late. His hand was there, and he was cupping her, pressing into her, rubbing his thumb against her, making it worse, making her hotter than she'd ever been in her life.

"No, sweetheart, don't fight me. Let me...let me. Spread your legs for me....that's it. Oh, Rachel, you're so wet, so swollen, so ready for me."

He lifted the nightgown with his other hand, slowly, by degrees, until it was above her waist, all the time praising her as he stated in no uncertain terms what he intended to do. With reverence and awe, he kissed her belly, soft, little kisses that began at her navel and descended to the core of her womanhood. He tasted her, then, with the tip of his tongue, breathing in her woman's perfume as he laved and soothed her.

Her hips rose to greet him, yet Rachel turned her face away, pushing herself into the pillow as far as her body would allow. She felt as if she were falling headfirst off a rugged cliff with murderous rocks below. Her legs fell apart of their own volition as her body rejoiced in the feel of his mouth, his tongue on her heated flesh.

It came on her too quickly, so much so that she wasn't prepared for it. Her body tensed and a moan she had been trying to tamp down erupted as a long, mournful sound escaped her lips. She grabbed the edge of the pillow and pulled it against her face as she twisted her body from him.

"Look at me," he said. She shook her head. "Rachel, look at me."

"I can't."

"Yes, you can. Just turn your head and open your eyes."

"No. I'm too embarrassed."

"Why?"

"Because of what you said."

"My words embarrass you?"

She nodded. "And me."

"Your reaction to me? Don't be embarrassed, be thrilled." He reached up and forcibly turned her head toward him. "I am."

"You are?"

"Can't you tell?" he asked, rubbing his hardness against her thigh. She stared into his eyes, hers two wide pools of gray. "I want you so much," he whispered. "Do you want me, too, Rachel? Tell me, do you?"

"Yes..." The word was drawn out on a hiss.

He cupped a protective palm around the tiny mound on her abdomen. "I don't want to do anything to hurt you."

"You won't."

"You'll tell me."

"Yes."

She turned to him then, opened her arms and wrapped them around his neck. She took his weight easily as he moved over her, entering her slowly, by degrees, allowing her body to adjust to him. Rachel tilted her hips forward in urgent welcome, loving the feel of him as he filled her inch by inch. She had never been filled like this... Oh, yes, she had... once before.

"Oh, Rachel..." He moaned her name in her ear as he buried himself fully into her. "Don't move."

She gently scraped his back with her nails, reveling in the shudder that shook his body as he pulled out almost all the way before rejoining them again...and again...and again.

And then she felt him tense, the muscles of his back and buttocks hardened under her hands. "Yes..." she urged as she felt his release bathe her insides with his liquid heat. "Oh, Reid, yes..."

She savored the feel of his weight on her body, hugging him close to her as she wrapped her legs around his.

Reid lifted his head and stared down at her. A slow smile creased his lips and his eyes crinkled in the firelight. "I'm too heavy for you."

"No, you're not."

"Yes, I am," he said, and rolled away from her.

She turned to face him, glad that he wasn't running off to another room, hoping that he'd spend the night with her here in this bed, wondering what she would have to do to make that happen.

He touched the tip of her nose with his finger. "What are you thinking about?" he asked.

"I was just wondering."

"About what?"

"About this *consummation* thing. Are we officially married now?" she asked.

Reid let out a laugh that seemed to come from his toes. He pulled her to him and kissed her soundly on the lips with a loud smack. "Yes, Rachel, rest assured. I believe we are *very* officially married now."

Rachel smiled, and sat up in the bed. "But you're not absolutely sure?"

Reid eyed her curiously as she moved toward him, then straddled him.

"What do you think you're doing?" he asked, a pleased but puzzled grin on his face.

For an answer, Rachel leaned forward and kissed him thoroughly. His arms reached up and wrapped around her waist. "You're right," he said, staring into her eyes. "Maybe once more," he whispered against her lips, "just to be on the safe side…."

Seven

"Where is he?" Trudy asked as she extricated herself from Rachel's welcoming hug.

"He's out back, mowing the lawn," Rachel answered.

"He's what?"

Rachel laughed. "You heard me. He's mowing the lawn. Actually, it's more like trimming the rain forest. There's so much growth back there. He's been at it for the past two weeks."

And what two weeks they had been. It was late September, with a lazy, hazy Indian summer full upon them. Rachel pinched herself each morning to be sure that she was truly here, living this dream.

After they'd made love on their wedding night, she'd awakened alone in her bed having slept most of the morning away. The smell of fresh-brewed coffee had lured her downstairs to find Reid puttering around the kitchen cleaning up after what appeared to have been an attempt to make blueberry muffins from scratch.

The sight had endeared him to her, adding to her confusion about the night before, a night of lovemaking so intense, so fulfilling, she wished it had never ended. The passionate woman she'd claimed not to know had once again miraculously materialized the moment he'd touched her, and each day that had passed since, Rachel waited in anticipation of a repeat performance.

But there had been none.

Reid had not returned to her bed. He was polite, kind, but reserved enough not to come too close to her, careful not to touch her even with the most ordinary human contact.

Yet he was very attentive to her needs. Together they had searched and found an obstetrician with whom she felt comfortable. It had even been his suggestion to sign up for childbirth preparation classes.

So, other than the fact that he physically kept his distance, Rachel had no complaints. At first, she'd been on pins and needles around him, but now, she was settling in to a kind of domestic routine.

It was almost as if they were truly married. Almost.

"This is unbelievable," Trudy said as she glanced out the kitchen bay window at Reid on the rider mower. "I wish I had a camera."

"He's really into this," Rachel said as she moved alongside Trudy at the window. "Every morning he goes to the hardware store in town to buy some other garden tool. The shopkeeper is so thrilled with him, he even delivered Reid's last order personally."

Reid spotted Trudy and Rachel, waved, and brought the mower to a halt. "He actually looks . . . happy," Trudy said softly.

Rachel turned to her. "You seem surprised. You're the one who told him to *live*."

"But I didn't think he knew how."

"Look who's here!" Reid wiped his sneakers on the doormat before proceeding into the kitchen to greet Trudy with a big hug.

"Ugh," she said, pulling away from him. "You're all sweaty. And you smell like—" she sniffed the air near him with great exaggeration "—grass."

Reid laughed and hugged her again. "Great, isn't it?"

"I hate grass. You should build a patio," she suggested. "Better yet, concrete the whole yard."

"What brings you up here?" he asked.

"It's Friday. You told me to bring the papers that needed to be signed when I visited."

"It's Friday already?" he asked Rachel.

"Yes, already."

Rachel reached up to pick grass out of his hair. He jumped back, but not before she'd made contact. She noted Trudy's curious expression, but said nothing as she dropped the cuttings into the trash.

"So, you two," Trudy began, her glance moving from Rachel to Reid. "How's it going?"

"Great!"

"Wonderful!"

Trudy nodded. "I see. Happy to hear it."

"How are things at the office?" Reid asked, feigning interest.

"Busy. The phones haven't stopped."

"Is that so?" He asked.

"Well, you must have known this leave of absence thing would cause a stir. Not to mention your marriage. The city is littered with more than a few broken hearts, Reid."

Reid looked from Trudy to Rachel. "She's exaggerating."

"Is she?"

"Yes."

"*No* broken hearts, Reid?" Rachel asked, blindsided by the intense wave of green that washed over her.

"None that I know of."

"How about that little blonde from Long Island?" Trudy asked, enjoying this unexpected but thoroughly amusing byplay between her best friend and employer.

"I don't know any blonde from Long Island," he said, giving Trudy a stern shut-your-mouth look.

"Sure you do. The one you squired to all those charity events this past year. Tiffany What's-her-name. She's been calling every day. On your private line, I might add. She refuses to take Charlotte's word for it and has been demanding to speak to you personally. I told Charlotte to give her this number—"

"Don't you dare," Reid said.

"But Charlotte wouldn't anyway." Trudy became serious. "You really should make a formal statement or something, Reid. People are talking about who this mysterious bride really is. All kinds of rumors are starting. You should bring Rachel to town and nip them in the bud."

Reid nodded slowly. Trudy had a point. While he didn't want to share Rachel or this life with anyone right now, he knew his business associates well enough to understand that they wouldn't rest until he showed himself with Rachel at his side. Until that time, they'd speculate and blow every small truth completely out of proportion. For Rachel's sake, and his own, not to mention the baby's, he'd be well advised to make a big splash of it, show off a bit, a debut, so to speak, of his bride to the swells of New York.

"Okay. We'll do it."

"Do what?" Rachel asked, not liking the determined look in his eye, particularly when she had the distinct feeling whatever it was he was planning centered around her.

"A party," he said. "Nothing too big. Just the right people. At the town house. I'll call Charlotte. She'll know who to invite."

"A party for what?" Rachel asked.

"Not what, Rachel. Who. You. We'll do it right. We'll introduce my bride to the world."

"Good idea," Trudy said.

"I don't see the need—"

"But there is, Rachel," Reid said. "When the baby comes, I don't want any questions, any doubts. An official introduction now will save a lot of speculation later."

Of course, Rachel thought. The baby. She placed her hand against her stomach as was fast becoming an unconscious habit. Reid would want to be sure everyone knew and accepted that the child was his. As it was, they'd be counting on their fingers when the happy event took place. He'd want to be sure no matter the math, there would be no question of parentage.

She understood his motivation. Growing up as he had, he would be doubly sensitive to that kind of talk. But the whole idea of a party to show her off was daunting to say the least. She wanted no part of it, yet knew she would go through with it with a smile on her face.

For his sake.

Because he needed this.

And with each passing day, his need was becoming hers.

God help her, but she was falling in love with him.

"If you think it's what we should do, of course I'll go along..." Rachel said.

"Then it's settled," Reid said as he strode toward the hall. "Trudy, why don't you change out of those city clothes and relax while I shower? We'll go over those papers later."

"Sure thing, Reid," Trudy said, leaning forward in her seat, watching as he disappeared before turning to Rachel. "*What* is going on?"

Rachel stared at her hands in her lap. "Nothing's going on."

"Bull. The two of you can't keep your eyes off each other when either of you thinks the other's not looking, then Reid almost jumps out of his skin when you try to touch him."

"Ridiculous."

"Don't tell me that. I make my living being observant, and the two of you are walking on eggs around each other. Now tell me, what gives? I thought you'd been sleeping with him—"

"Once."

"What? Only once? In two weeks? What's wrong? Don't you feel all right?"

Rachel stood and began pacing. "I feel fine! I've never felt better in my life. I know you're supposed to be sick all the time when you're pregnant, but I'm not. I feel wonderful."

"Then what's the problem?"

"Reid's the problem. He won't touch me...and he won't let me touch him."

"Is there anything wrong with *him?*"

"No." Rachel's eyes glazed as memories of their lovemaking swirled around her, and her voice softened. "Not a thing."

"Spare me the details," Trudy said. She tapped her forefinger to her lips. "Then I wonder why he's being so remote? I mean, why make love at all if he had no intention of continuing the relationship?"

"Consummation."

"What?"

"He wanted us to consummate the marriage."

"He *said* that?"

"Uh-huh. In those words."

"Lord, sometimes his past catches up with him."

"What do you mean?" Rachel asked as she stopped pacing. "The orphanage?"

"Yeah. *And* the nuns. *And* the guilt. *Consummate.* What a word! For a liberal guy, he's got a very rigid set of rules he applies to himself."

"So what do you think I should do?"

Trudy looked at her. "Why, seduce him, of course!"

"You must be kidding."

"No, I'm perfectly serious. He's obviously waiting for you to make the next move."

"That's insane," Rachel said, shaking her head. "He certainly wasn't shy the night we... well, it's just crazy to think he's waiting for *me.*"

Trudy stood and came over to Rachel, taking her by the shoulders. "Don't you see? He suggested 'consummating' the marriage and you agreed. He thinks you've just done your duty, and now that the deed is done, there's no need to repeat it. Unless, of course, you want to."

"Do you really think that's it?"

"Do you have any better ideas?" Trudy asked.

"None."

"Then what have you got to lose?"

Rachel placed the palm of her hand against her abdomen and pressed the small round mound that was becoming more pronounced by the day. "Nothing," she said, *and everything...*

Trudy's Friday visits became routine, but she never failed to leave early the next morning despite Reid's insistence that she spend the weekend. He'd wanted Trudy to stay as a buffer between him and Rachel. Being alone with her all the time was wearing him down, but he'd vowed the night they'd made love that he wouldn't push himself on her again.

After all, she hadn't wanted to marry him to begin with, she hadn't been able to commit herself to him for any length of time, and she hadn't even wanted to make love with him at all until he'd brought up the necessity. It was pretty obvious to him that she needed time to get to know him better, and he had tried his best to be as nonthreatening as possible ever since.

But that didn't stop him from wanting her. She'd claimed she hadn't remembered their first time together, but he seriously doubted she could make the same statement about their wedding night. As quiet and reserved as she was in ordinary daily life, Rachel seemed to have the ability to metamorphose into an uninhibited sexual being when the lights went down.

He wondered if she was conscious of the change or even realized how absolutely crazy she drove him. Time and again, she'd taken him all the way to the brink and back until he'd become as conditioned as Pavlov's dog—all he needed from her was a heated look, a whispered word, the slightest touch to send him over the edge.

So he didn't touch her, not at all, not even by accident. Because if he did, he wouldn't be able to stop. He thought about it all the time—what he would do if she came to him. He'd start by undressing her, cupping her breasts, suckling those large silver-dollar nipples of hers until they were puckered and hard on his tongue. He'd rub against her just before burying himself deep inside her warmth... and then she'd move, taking him with her to that place in time and space that only she seemed able to create for him.

Gripping the weed-whacker he'd bought that morning, he turned it on with shaky hands. His body was hard and tight with thoughts too erotic to have a basis in reality. She wasn't coming to him, at least not like that, and he'd better learn to live with that fact. He forced his mind to think of other things—the yard, the grass, this small cove in the corner by the pines that he wanted to clear—anything, everything, except Rachel....

But all this self-restraint was getting to him. She had no idea how she looked to him as she ambled around the house in all states of dress. Her body was changing every day in ways that enticed, lured, beckoned. She was like a fruit ripening to perfection before his eyes, and more than anything he wanted to taste her. All the time. Day, night, and those twilight times in between that were the worst of all.

You could fall in love with her...

Trudy's words kept replaying in his head. He hadn't thought such a thing possible, not for him, not for Reid James, the Invincible...but a small, niggling worry had taken up residence in his brain. What if he did fall in love with her? What if he *did*... and she left him?

He couldn't explain the feeling of panic that overcame him with that thought. He had spent his entire adult life—ever since he was sixteen and he'd discovered his true parentage—negating his emotions, his expectations, his hopes and desires. Things, not people, became the focus of his life, and while he was willing to give himself over to their child when it was born, he found the idea of trusting a woman with his love totally incomprehensible.

But with Rachel, he was coming very, very close to that reality. Which explained the fear he'd had the first night he'd met her. His instincts had recognized the danger of her from the first even if his conscious mind had not. Like it or not, Rachel scared the hell out of him.

He ran the weed-whacker along the rim of thick pines that served as a natural fence dividing the yard from the woods that lay beyond. A mixture of grass and weeds swirled up at him, sticking to his damp skin, bits and pieces entangling themselves in his chest hair and every other available nook and cranny on his body.

The physical activity felt good, better than any workout in a gym. He loved the scent of fall in the air, he loved the light October breeze that bit at his back, he loved the heat of the day and the coolness of the night. He knew why this place had called out to him, why he'd impulsively bought it on the spot. He felt alive here, reborn, part of the earth, the sky. . . and he'd never felt so free.

He wanted it to last forever, this idyll, this time with Rachel in between the real world and the baby to come.

But life was intruding.

The party was tonight. He and Rachel had decided to spend the day in Connecticut and drive down late in the afternoon. It was just as well they were leaving. Maybe it *was* the air here, or being alone on his own property with his own woman. Whatever the cause, he felt charged, energized, ready for anything, and so powerfully male that he knew his testosterone level must be at an all time high.

Rachel, stay away. . .

But, of course, she wouldn't. Even now from the corner of his eye he watched her progress as she crossed the lawn, moving slowly, steadily toward him. Maybe like him, she couldn't keep away. That thought warmed him even as he dismissed it from his mind as impossible.

"Hi," she said with a smile. "I brought ice water."

Reid turned off the machine and laid it down. "Thanks," he said, taking the proffered plastic cup and drinking thirstily.

"Are you ready for some lunch?" she asked.

"Almost."

"I've put a ham-and-cheese quiche in the oven. Would you like some?"

"What I'd like is a double-bacon-and-cheese sirloin burger."

Rachel grinned. "A little hungry, Reid?"

Reid wiped the back of his hand across his mouth and held out the empty cup to her. "A little starved, Rachel."

She took the cup from him, careful not to touch him in any way as she did so. Their eyes met briefly. "I'll see what I can do," she said as she stuffed her other hand into her pocket and wiggled her bare toes in the grass.

Reid's gaze moved slowly up and down her body. She wore an oversize shirt with a tube top underneath and cut-offs, which were unsnapped, a small concession to her expanding waistline. "Why don't you start without me," he said, fighting an urge to insinuate his fingers into that opening.

"I don't mind waiting for you."

Reid looked down at himself. "I need to clean up. I'm a mess," he said, wiping his hands down the sides of his shorts and sending the grass and dirt flying.

"Here," she said, dropping the plastic cup on the grass. "Let me help."

Rachel began brushing the stray specks of grass off his legs, up toward his arms. "Lord, you *are* a mess," she said with a short laugh that caught in her throat as she reached his chest and realized he'd stopped moving.

She raised her head. The look in his golden green eyes brought home her error immediately. She'd touched him. Although the rule was unspoken, it was still a rule, and she knew it.

She looked down at her right hand which was entwined in his chest hair. Her fingers slowly recoiled. "Sorry," she said softly. "I didn't mean—"

Reid grabbed hold of her wrist before she could pull away. "Rachel," he said, "look at me."

She did. His eyes had changed to a brilliant, fire green, filled with desire and a longing that she wholeheartedly shared, but his touch contradicted the look. She could tell by his grip that he was about to let her go, push her away from him, toward the house.

But she didn't want to go, so she decided to test Trudy's theory that he was waiting for her to make the first move. She inched closer to him, raised herself up onto her tiptoes and brushed her mouth against his.

"What do you think you're doing?" he asked.

"Kissing you."

"I'll get you all dirty."

She rubbed the palms of her hands into his sweaty chest before reaching up to link her arms around his neck. "I don't care."

She slipped her tongue between his lips, tentatively at first, then bolder as his arms came up around her. Spinning her around, he returned her kiss, angling his head for better access to her lips, her neck, that hollow behind her ear that drew the tip of his tongue toward it like a magnet.

He knew he had to stop now or not at all. "Rachel . . . don't start this."

"Why?" she asked as she tugged at her tube top, pulling it down. Her breasts spilled out, and she rubbed herself against his chest, eliciting a very satisfying moan from his throat.

"Because." He gave in and cupped her, cradling one full breast in each hand as he carefully kneaded her softness with his palms.

She reached up and scratched her fingers through his chest hair. "Why, because?"

"Because...I...can't...won't...stop." With almost no effort on his part, her zipper separated, her cutoffs becoming a gaping open invitation to dip his fingers inside.

"I don't want you to stop."

"What do you want?" He insinuated his hand into her bikini panties. "To make love . . . right here?"

Rachel wriggled against his hand. She gripped his shoulders. As his fingers found their mark, she shuddered. "Lovely spot..."

He flicked the tiny bud of flesh slowly, back and forth and felt her melt in his hand. "Oh, sweetheart, I agree..."

Before she knew what hit her, Rachel was flat on her back in the grass. "Is this how you want it?" He stroked her deeply, steadily, until she was wet and swollen.

"Yes...no..." she whispered. "I want more."

Reid's fingers stilled. Carefully he extricated his hand from her panties and splayed his palm across her abdomen. He held his hand firmly there at the spot where their child grew and stared into her eyes. Myriad thoughts and emotions bounced around his head like an erratic, out-of-control pinball.

Rachel placed her hand on top of his and pressed down. "I want you."

"Say that again," he asked.

Rachel lifted herself up onto one elbow. Reaching into his waistband, she touched him intimately. He was gratifyingly hard and ready for her. She smiled, a thoroughly female smile of triumph. "You, Reid, I want you. Right here, right now..."

He leaned forward, and she met him halfway. Her mouth watered in anticipation of the heat she knew she'd find there. And then they kissed. Their mouths melded so naturally, as if they were two halves to a whole. She opened herself to his heat, to his touch.

And, oh, did he know how to touch. As Reid's fingers found her again, her legs parted and her hips rose in welcome. Her body liquefied as in tandem his tongue filled her mouth and his fingers stroked her intimately.

His mouth moved to her chin, her cheeks, her neck, nipping his way around her face like a crazed, starved man eating his first meal in days.

He marked her neck, sucking her skin, grazing his teeth across her flesh until he found the first large, pouting nipple. He opened his mouth wide to accept all of it. Gently, tenderly, he laved the hardened bud. She felt his hot suckling deep in her womb, a tingling fireball that shot down with arrow accuracy to the core of her desire, and she blossomed open for him.

Rachel took him in her hand, stroking his length, width, and hardness. She ran the pad of her finger across the tip of his arousal and was rewarded with a bead of wetness.

Reid was over the top, gone, beyond reason. His body was crying out to him, beseeching him to take her, desperate to be inside her, demanding release.

It all became too much and not enough for both of them at the same time. Together they shed each other's clothes and came together.

"Am I hurting you?" he asked as he eased himself into her more deeply.

"No, oh, no, Reid, please, don't stop...do it...all the way."

With a forward thrust of his hips he joined them fully. He held himself off her with his arms, one hand on either side of her head. Rachel rubbed her hands up and down his sides around to his buttocks as she bent her knees and lifted her legs high to cradle his hips.

"Yes-s..." she hissed as he pulled out almost all the way before sliding back into her again and again and again.

His mouth came down on hers. The kiss was long, wet and bittersweet as his body pumped his hopes, his dreams, his love into hers.

She felt so good, so filled, so perfectly *right* joined to him with the green earth against her back and the blue sky above her head. She gave herself up to her senses, shutting her eyes to all but her inner voice, the one that was calling to her, crooking its finger to her, inviting her to give her very self over to the pleasure that awaited her.

She floated toward that light, her hunger for more of him, all of him, making her greedy. Her hips lunged up to meet him as her insides contracted once, twice, again and again. She began to chant his name. "Reid . . . Reid . . . Reid . . ."

"Rachel . . ." His hoarse whisper grazed her ear. "I . . . can't . . . hold . . . off . . ."

"Don't . . ."

"Rachel . . . sweet . . . Rachel . . ."

He bathed her with his warm essence, and she criss-crossed her legs high across his back to keep him still, to absorb the aftershocks, to do something now, in this fantastic, fantasy moment, that she knew would not be possible in the real world: hold him to her forever.

Their eyes met. His hand moved from her neck as he brushed away bits of grass from her face and hair. "Rachel . . ."

"Yes . . ."

"I—"

"Mr. James? Yoo-hoo! Mr. James? Are you back there? I have those hedge trimmers you ordered . . ."

They jumped up at the same time. Reid hopped into his shorts as he muttered a string of expletives. Rachel slipped into her cutoffs, pulled up her tube top and straightened her shirt in record time. By the time the owner of the hardware store had found them in the cove, their clothes were righted even if their expressions were a little strange.

"There you are!" Mr. McCaffrey called with a wave of his arm. He tipped his baseball cap, which had Mac's Hardware embroidered across the brim, to Rachel and, with a nod, said, "Ma'am." Then he looked to Reid. "I was just in the neighborhood and thought I'd drop these off to you. Save you a trip to town."

"Well, thank you, Mr. McCaffrey, you didn't have to do that," Reid said, accepting the tool.

"No trouble, no trouble at all." He grinned broadly, looking from Reid to Rachel, then back again. "You been using that weed-whacker I sold you?"

"Uh . . . why, yes, I have," Reid said.

"That shouldn't be kicking up grass like that. Look at you two! Grass and dirt all over you! Let me take a look at that."

Mr. McCaffrey grabbed the weed-whacker and turned it left and right as he examined it for defects. Reid caught Rachel's eye over his head and smiled. She bit her lip to stop her laughter from bubbling forth.

"I think I'll go check on lunch," she said.

Mr. McCaffrey's head shot up. "Oh, lordy, I meant to tell you. Saw some smoke drifting out of your kitchen window as I passed—"

"My quiche!" Rachel exclaimed as she ran toward the house.

The two men stared after her.

"Quiche?" Mr. McCaffrey asked.

"It's kind of like a pie."

"Doesn't sound like much of a lunch to me."

"It's not."

Mr. McCaffrey shook his head. "My wife was the same way when we first got married. Don't worry about it. Brides need to learn how to satisfy a man's appetite."

Reid watched Rachel's hips sway as she hurried up the back steps and into the house. "Oh, she's learning, Mr. McCaffrey. She's learning just fine."

Eight

They were beyond fashionably late for their own party.

Charlotte greeted Reid and Rachel at the door with a strained smile that all but said "Thank God, you're finally here!" The group of curious guests she had painstakingly assembled applauded the couple as they made their grand entrance into the living room of Reid's town house.

The crowd rushed them, forcing the ever-efficient Charlotte to orchestrate a receiving line. All eyes were drawn to Reid James's bride, and Rachel felt as if she were an exotic new panda bear on display at the Bronx Zoo.

As they were paraded in front of her, she graciously shook each hand, not even trying to remember the names after the first dozen had passed. Each guest smiled as they congratulated her on her marriage, their eyes surreptitiously looking her up and down before probing deeply into hers as if to determine what unique quality she possessed that had caused Reid to marry her in the first place.

To make matters worse, everyone had a comment about their lateness. Reid made an excuse about the traffic, but Rachel's face burned with embarrassment as she was sure that each person whose eyes met hers categorically knew exactly what they had been doing that had so detained them.

Yet despite the awkwardness she was feeling, Rachel was on a natural high. These people, this party, only served as background noise to what was going on in her head. An awareness had blossomed between her and Reid after their interlude in the cove, and though they didn't speak of it, a new level had been reached in their relationship.

It might seem silly to some, but to Rachel, the fact that she could touch him at will was a major breakthrough in what had become an almost unbearable atmosphere of tension in the house. Amazingly, once she'd taken the first step to shatter that taboo, Reid seemed totally unable to keep his hands off her for the rest of the day.

It was no wonder that showering and dressing for the evening had become something else entirely when, in a hurry, she'd asked Reid to help her with the back zipper.

Instead of quickly handling the task at hand, he'd leisurely touched her with his fingertips, tracing the line of her spine as if they had all the time in the world. When he'd reached her neck, he'd kissed it, his breath fanning the soft hairs at her nape and causing chills to run up and down her entire body. The thought of fastening her dress seem to fade as he'd reached inside, cupping and caressing her breasts from behind.

Rachel had leaned back into him and melted in his arms as he pressed himself into her. As she'd felt the strength of his arousal against her buttocks, he'd whispered her name in her ear, a prayerful entreaty that left no doubt in her mind what he wanted, what he needed, and where all of this was going to end.

After that, all rational thought was lost.

They'd made love again, this time standing up against the door, though her bed was only steps away. It had been a wild, passionate, almost frenzied coupling, as if they hadn't touched each other for weeks instead of only hours.

Her dress had become hopelessly wrinkled, and Rachel, having no other, had had to iron it. Which left her no time at all to fiddle with her hair. She'd had to settle for a quick brushing on the run out the front door. Applying her makeup in the car using the visor mirror as they'd sped down the New England thruway was an adventure to be sure. She bet they hit every crack, crevice and known pothole just as she applied each stroke of shadow to her eyelids and lipstick to her lips.

She knew she looked as if she'd been put together with spit and glue, and was equally sure that everyone she now faced had exactly the same opinion.

So much for her debut.

She sighed as she adjusted the scarf around her neck, a last-minute addition to her too low, too-much-bosom-showing dress she'd thought had looked so sophisticated when she'd tried it on in the little shop in town.

She looked up at Reid as he pulled her toward a group of his colleagues and business associates. He smiled down at her, a possessive arm around her waist, completely oblivious to her distress. He, of course, looked perfect. His blond hair was combed back, but, as usual, it fell down onto his forehead. His emerald eyes stood out like beacons in a face evenly tanned from his daily yard activities in the sun. His Italian designer suit was impeccably turned out. Even his shoes were shined.

Rachel smiled at each guest in the group, convinced by now that they all thought her a poor imitation of what a wife of Reid James should be. She grimaced to herself. Just wait till they heard she was pregnant.

Standing by Reid's side as he began to discuss business, her eyes searched over every head for Trudy, but the crush of people made it virtually impossible for her to find her friend. She laid in wait with an occasional glance around the room, and finally spotted her coming out of the kitchen. She waved and motioned to Trudy to meet her upstairs. Making her excuses to Reid, she weaved through the crowd on her way up to the master bedroom.

Trudy entered the room behind Rachel, who headed straight for the lounge, sat and kicked off her shoes.

"So this is the infamous *white* room..." Trudy said, followed by a nasal interpretation of the "Twilight Zone" theme.

"Trudy..."

Trudy stood in the middle of the room, hand on hip, surveying the area. "Oh, let me have some fun. I've never been up here."

"I should hope not." Rachel's head snapped up as a thought struck her. "Have you ever wanted to?"

"Get it on with Reid?" Trudy asked. Rachel nodded. "Sure, at first. But the boss thing was a no-no." She shrugged. "Who in this town hasn't thought about Reid that way? There are probably at least twenty females downstairs right now who have had the same fantasy at one time or another over the years."

"But how many have *experienced* it in fact?" Rachel asked, intrigued.

"A few, I'm sure. I only know of one."

Rachel was incredulous. "One of his old girlfriends is downstairs?"

"The blonde. From Long Island. She got someone to bring her. I guess she couldn't resist getting a close look at you."

Rachel racked her brain to place the woman. "I've met several blondes tonight. Reid didn't seem particularly interested in any of them."

"Reid isn't." Trudy's eyes met Rachel's. "God, you really don't know, do you?"

"Know what?"

"The man only has eyes for you, girl. He's crazy about you."

"Don't say that. It's not true."

"Why shouldn't I say it? It *is* true."

"No, it's not. Don't you think I'd know it if he were? Don't you think he'd say something?"

"No, I don't. He doesn't know how. That's going to be up to you. You're going to have to drag it out of him."

"I don't want to talk about it," Rachel said emphatically. She couldn't allow herself to think that way, to think that he might be feeling things for her... things she was feeling for him. Because if she started to believe that, and it wasn't true... if he really didn't...

Trudy came over and put an arm around her. "There's no need for you to be jealous, Rachel. He married you."

"Jealous? You must be joking! Really, Trudy," Rachel said, her stomach twisting with a profound, deep jealousy that she couldn't control for the life of her. "I only wanted to know which woman he dated."

"I'll point her out to you when we go back down."

"Fine."

Rachel stood and walked over to the window. She stared out at the city down below. "What a great view," she said softly as she rested her hand on her abdomen and pressed lightly.

Trudy came up behind her. "It's a beautiful room."

"Yes. It is."

"Do you still hate it?" Trudy asked as Rachel went back to the lounge.

Rachel sat, looked around, and shrugged. "It's growing on me."

"That's not all," Trudy said as she hovered over her, picking something out of Rachel's hair.

"What?"

"This." Trudy held up a small twig. "I can't wait to hear how this got into your hair."

Rachel felt herself blush to her roots.

"Look at your face! What happened? Did you take my advice? Did you seduce him?" When Rachel didn't answer, Trudy persisted, "You *did,* didn't you?"

Rachel tried to suppress a guilty smile, but Trudy was too quick.

"Did it work?"

Rachel reached up and slowly pulled the scarf away from her neck. Trudy's eyes lit up. "Oh, my God, look at your neck!"

"It's not that bad," Rachel said, replacing the scarf to cover the red marks Reid's passion had left behind.

"Not bad? You come to your debut party with a big fat hickey on your neck, and you say it's not that bad?"

"It's not a hickey."

"Oh, no?" Trudy pulled off the scarf. "Then what is it?"

"Just a mark."

"I don't believe it! Reid gave you a hickey! Where did you do it?"

"Trudy!"

"Come on, tell me." Then her eyes lit up. "In the grass! He's always mowing that stupid lawn. That's where you got the twig in your hair. This is so fabulous!"

"What's fabulous?"

The two women turned in unison as Reid stepped through the door. Rachel's stomach flipped as he walked toward her. It happened every time she saw him, but it still took her by surprise.

"Ah, uh...Rachel's dress," Trudy said as she draped the scarf back around Rachel's neck. "I was just saying how fabulous it was."

He came up beside Rachel. "Yes," he said softly, caressing her cheek with his palm. "She looks particularly radiant tonight. Everyone has commented on it."

Reid couldn't take his eyes off her. He knew he was making a class-A fool out of himself tonight, but he couldn't help it. When he'd looked around the room and couldn't find her, a wave of sheer panic had attacked him. *Just like the last time...* he'd thought, remembering how he'd searched this entire town house from top to bottom like a madman looking for her that night she'd disappeared on him.

The thought that that could ever happen again was terrifying. He couldn't imagine life without talking to her, touching her, being with her anymore, life without the hope and challenge that their child would bring to them. She had no idea, he knew, what he was feeling or what he was thinking. He didn't know how to tell her; he, who knew how to close any business deal ever created, could not find the words to tell this woman how he felt about her, what she meant to him.

He could only show her, and hope and pray she understood.

Their eyes met. For a long moment he scanned her face, the silence stretching until Trudy's fake cough brought their attention back to the fact that they were not alone.

"I'll see you two back downstairs," Trudy said with a smile and a wink to Rachel as she disappeared behind Reid and out the door.

"Are you feeling all right?" Reid asked once Trudy had left.

"Yes, I'm fine," Rachel said.

He extended his hand. "Then I think we'd better get back down to our guests."

"Of course," she said.

She slipped into her shoes as she reached for his hand. His fingers closed over hers and their eyes met again. Rachel's already flushed face turned an ever-brighter red.

"Are you sure you're feeling all right?" he asked. "You look flushed."

"No. . . really, I'm fine. It's just a bit warm in here."

"Take off the scarf," he suggested.

"No, it's okay."

"Rachel, why be uncomfortable? Take it off." He tugged at the end of the scarf and it fell away.

Reid's eyes lasered in on the mark on her neck.

"That's why," she said.

"Did I do that?"

She nodded.

"I'm sorry," he said, tracing the love bite with his fingertips before cupping the back of her neck and pulling her closer to him. "That's a lie," he whispered, his lips only inches away from her mouth. "I'm not sorry at all."

He kissed her, gently, tenderly, thoroughly. "Let's stay up here," he suggested.

"We can't . . . They'll come looking for us . . ."

"They wouldn't dare . . ."

"Charlotte . . ."

Reid broke away and blew out a breath of frustration. "You're right. Charlotte would dare." He lifted the scarf and rewrapped it around her neck. "Let's go."

He led her down the stairs and back into the crowd. Almost immediately he was pulled away by a group of business associates anxious to hear what he had to say about some new stock investment they had made. Rachel good-naturedly waved him on as she attempted to locate Charlotte and find out the estimated time of the party's demise.

She was tired and exhilarated at the same time. The events of the day had taken her on an emotional roller-coaster ride. Reid couldn't have been more loving than he had been this afternoon. Rachel basked in the power of her femininity, proud of what she had accomplished by going to him today. She smiled to herself. Bless Trudy for her suggestion.

A small ray of hope pierced her heart that perhaps Trudy was right, that there could be more to this marriage than just a convenient arrangement for them to share the baby, that perhaps in time he could fall in love with her . . . the way she feared she was already in love with him.

"Some punch, Rachel?"

Rachel turned to find Jules Laraby holding a glass out to her. "Thanks," she said, accepting the drink. She hesitated as she lifted it to her lips. "It isn't spiked, is it?" she asked with a smile, knowing that he was one of the very few people who knew exactly how she had come to be here in the first place.

"No. It's just juice." Jules laughed. "I poured it myself."

Rachel sipped the fruity liquid. "Thank you."

"You're welcome," he said. "So, how do you like the party?"

"It's very nice. Charlotte has done a wonderful job."

"She is very efficient," he said softly. "But . . . she isn't Reid."

Rachel looked up sharply. "What's that supposed to mean, Jules?"

Jules shrugged. "Just what it sounds like. Charlotte is a great assistant, but she's no Reid James. Short-term, she can do a competent job of running things, but in the long run . . . well, let's just say the company will suffer without him."

"Reid's only taking a leave of absence. He's not retiring."

"So he says. But the talk is, he's giving it all up." Jules looked pointedly at Rachel. "For you."

"That's absurd."

"I agree. But talk has a way of becoming a self-fulfilling prophecy in and of itself. The longer he stays away, the harder it will be to step back in. He'll lose his credibility. . . his clout."

"And you don't want to see that happen, do you, Jules?"

"Of course not. No one does. Least of all Reid himself. I don't think he realizes what this little escapade will cost him in the end."

Rachel bristled. She supposed she and the baby constituted the *little escapade.* "Reid is a very bright man. He hasn't built the empire he has without knowing what he is doing. I'm sure he has a plan."

Jules smiled. "You're right, of course," he said, pointing in Reid's direction. "Just look at him. He's enjoying every bit of this evening. He's back where he loves to be, wheeling and dealing, working the crowd as only he can. He won't be able to stay away for long."

Rachel's eyes followed Jules's as she watched Reid shake hands and move through the room. It was true. Reid was in his element here. He was alive, animated, wired—exactly as he'd been when she'd first met him. The man who mowed the lawn and pulled weeds in the backyard in Connecticut was someone else, too low-key to be this dynamic symbol of big business who worked the room before her now as if he were born to it.

How long would it be before he tired of this little game of playing house with her? Would it last through winter? Until the baby was born? When?

Jules's words echoed her thoughts. "By the time the first snow falls, he'll tire of all that rustic charm and he'll be back in the game, well-rested and raring to go." Jules rocked on his heels. "Besides, before we know it the baby will be due, and the contracted year will be almost over."

Rachel's eyes shot up. "What do you mean? We signed no contract."

Jules shrugged. "Signed or not, the terms still apply. You and Reid verbally agreed—in front of me as witness, no less." He patted her arm, and dropped his voice. "Don't worry, Rachel, Reid's as good as his word. He made it perfectly clear that there is nothing more important to him than this baby. He wants to keep you happy. After the year is up, you'll be free to go, just as you wished, just as was outlined in the nuptial agreement."

"Th-thank you for telling me that, Jules."

"Anytime you have any legal questions about your position, or, more importantly," he said softly, "the baby's—you just give me a call. I'll be more than happy to answer anything you may be uncertain about at any time."

"That's very kind of you."

"Hey! Anything for you and Reid. After all, don't forget, I'm your best man."

Rachel managed a small smile as Jules walked away, but her stomach was turning over and over at the implications of his words.

Nothing is more important to him than this baby.

Contract or no, she—as well as Reid—had an out once the baby was born. How stupid could she have been? Of course Reid would see to it that he was protected. He was a businessman first and foremost. Had she forgotten that his first action after meeting her was to have her investigated? Everything—every *single* thing he'd done had been calculated to get what he wanted. Her, yes, but first and foremost, the baby.

Not once had he indicated that he wanted any more from her. Not once had he even attempted to share anything about himself with her. While she prattled away telling him things about her childhood, her parents, her hopes and dreams for the baby, he remained politely silent. She'd tried a number of times to get him to talk about his early life, to talk about his feelings, but before the questions would even leave her lips, a stone wall would drop between them. It was as if he viewed this entire arrangement as too temporary to warrant any effort on his part to share himself.

He wants to keep you happy.

Did that include making love to her until she was senseless? Did that include making her fall so in love with him that she'd be too blind to see what he was orchestrating behind the scenes? Was it all an act? The house in the country, the decorating, the doctor's appointment, signing up for childbirth classes, *mowing* the lawn… Oh, God! How could she have been so stupid?

This was no marriage, this wasn't even a relationship. This was . . . nothing.

Rachel fought the tears that threatened to seep from behind her eyelids. Her hands began to shake and, with both hands, she brought the glass up to her lips, attempting but not succeeding to swallow the last of the fruit juice.

"You're a success."

She looked up at a beaming Charlotte. "Am I?"

"Well . . . yes . . . you are. Rachel? What's wrong?"

"Nothing." She took a deep, cleansing breath. "Nothing at all. It's a lovely party, Charlotte. You did a great job. Thank you for all your hard work."

Charlotte eyed her. "Are you sure you're all right? You're not feeling faint or anything?"

"No. I'm fine. Just tired, I guess."

"The crowd's beginning to get restless. The party will be breaking up soon. Once a few begin to leave, there will be a mass exodus. Are you staying the night here or returning to Connecticut?"

Rachel opened her mouth, then shut it. "I have no idea," she said finally. "I'd rather go back to Connecticut, but I suppose it's up to Reid. He's driving."

"Where am I driving?" Reid said as he came up behind her and wrapped his arms around her waist.

Rachel held herself as stiffly as possible. "To Connecticut?"

"Tonight?"

"If you don't mind?" Rachel said.

"I thought we'd stay here."

"I'd rather not."

Reid shrugged, then grinned good-naturedly. "I forgot." He looked at Charlotte. "She's got this thing about *white*. Okay. I guess I'll have enough energy left to make the ride."

"I'd say you could shoot the moon right now if you wanted to, Reid," Charlotte said.

"You're probably right. I'm charged."

"Speaking of which..." Charlotte began, "I see people milling about near the door. This may be the beginning of the end. Excuse me."

Reid dropped his arms from Rache's waist and pulled her to his side. "You're more at home here than in Connecticut, aren't you, Reid?" Rachel commented.

Reid turned her to face him. "I like to think I can be at home in both places."

"It's a nice thought," she said.

He looked puzzled. "Yes, it is. And a true one. What gives, Rachel?"

Rachel shook her head and forced herself to smile. Now was not the time nor the place to air her doubts about his intentions. She took his arm and was saved from having to answer him when Charlotte returned with guests who had come to say their goodbyes. Rachel played the gracious Mrs. Reid James to perfection, as expected.

The night was over, her debut complete, but she felt no triumph, only an emptiness in the center of her heart that she feared would never be filled.

"Thank you for tonight."

Rachel glanced at Reid from the corner of her eye. "You're welcome."

Reid started the engine of the car and backed out of the parking garage he kept in the city. Tonight was a night he'd remember always. He couldn't recall a time when he'd felt more personal satisfaction than he had as he'd walked into the party with Rachel on his arm. Nothing in his memory could compare to it, not even that moment when his father had tracked him down, acknowledged his existence for the first time, then asked him for a loan.

That had been sweet; this was better.

She looked beautiful, her long, dark hair and tanned skin in shimmering contrast to the formfitting cream-colored gown. He'd felt proud to present her as his wife, but it was more than that. There was a completeness inside him that was so fulfilling at times during the evening he'd had to fight to keep his emotions from surfacing.

He'd wanted to shout out loud about the baby to come, about their child that was nestled warm and growing bigger by the day inside his wife, his woman, his...

Rachel...

They'd made love today. She'd come to him just as he'd fantasized. It couldn't have been better if he'd written the script for the day himself. She'd been happy, he knew it, he felt it, so tuned in to her, he could anticipate every move, every word.

Until a short while ago. He pressed down harder on the accelerator as he drove toward the entrance onto the East River Drive. She'd made it clear that she wanted to return to Connecticut. He'd thought after today her aversion to his town house would have disappeared, but apparently that was not the case.

Something had happened between the time they'd spent in his bedroom to the time they were ready to leave. Suddenly something was very wrong. He could feel it emanating from her like an aura from hell. The sweet, pliant, loving Rachel was gone, and a cool, reserved, aloof angel had taken her place. Why?

"Tired?"

"Yes."

"Grumpy?"

"No."

"You seem grumpy."

Rachel sighed. He was trying to "cute" her out of her bad mood, and she wanted no part of it. They were alone now, there was no need to continue this "perfect couple" charade.

"Want to talk about it?" he asked.

"There's nothing to talk about."

"I think there is. Earlier today...tonight...you were fine. Now you're remote. What happened between then and now to change your mood? Didn't you like the party?"

"The party was wonderful. Charlotte did a wonderful job."

"Yes, she did, but that's not what I'm asking. Did you have a good time?"

"I did my duty."

"Your *duty?*"

"Yes. I played the part of Mrs. Reid James. I thought I did an excellent job of it."

Reid gritted his teeth. His insides were churning, and he had to take a second or two to rein himself in. "So. This is a game."

"Isn't it?"

"Not to me."

Rachel gave him a wry grin. "We're alone, Reid. You don't have to pretend anymore."

"I don't know what you're talking about, Rachel. What happened tonight?"

"Let's just say I had my eyes opened a bit."

"By?"

Rachel bit her lip. She had no desire to implicate Jules in any of this. He was only being friendly, and she'd already gotten him into trouble with Reid once before.

"The little blonde from Long Island," she lied, hoping she could divert him from the source of her true concerns. "She was there, wasn't she?"

"Tiffany? Who told you that? No, don't answer. It had to be Trudy."

"Don't blame her."

"She has a big mouth."

"She didn't invite the woman."

"No one did. She wrangled her way in."

"Just to see you."

"No, not me. You."

"Oh, that's right. The blushing bride."

"Perhaps the bitchy bride might be more appropriate."

Rachel's mouth formed an O. "How dare you call me that!"

"If the shoe fits..."

Rachel didn't answer. She was too angry, too hurt, too agitated to trust herself to speak. Her mind was in a turmoil and her hormones were raging. She knew she was being irrational, bouncing back and forth between loving him and hating him. She wanted to kiss him and tell him off at the same time.

But what could she really say to him anyway? That he had betrayed her? No, he had done everything he'd promised. He'd married her, moved her to Connecticut to live with him, taken care of her, and had not approached her sexually since they'd consummated the marriage—all of which she had agreed to.

Any further action had been executed on her part. She had been the one to seduce him today, touch him when she knew how he felt about being touched by her. She had been the one to initiate making love, outdoors no less, in the middle of the day. No healthy, red-blooded male would have turned her away, and Reid could not be expected to be the exception.

So he didn't love her, maybe he could *never* love her. He'd had a strange, disconnected childhood, which he chose not to share with her. Perhaps he was incapable of feeling that kind of emotion. What did she expect from him? A declaration of undying love because she'd rolled around in the grass with him?

She had to get a grip. She had to be as realistic about this marriage as he obviously was. They'd made a deal, and he was doing his damnedest to see it through. She could do no less. If nothing else, she owed it to the baby.

"Okay," she said finally, placing a protective hand on her abdomen.

"Okay, what?"

"You're right. I was being bitchy. I'm sorry. Let's forget it."

"I'd like to know why."

"Let's chalk it up to being pregnant. I guess I'm more touchy than I thought."

"About?"

"Parties in the city and blondes that want to check me out. Can we let it go now?"

"If that's what you want."

"That's what I want."

Reid glanced at her before returning his attention to the road. He was sure there was more to it than that, but her distraction was affecting him, as well. Had she meant what she said, that she was only doing her "duty," playing at being his wife? She was being sarcastic, but sometimes the truth was hidden in layers. No one knew that better than he.

He shook his head at his own naiveté. Here he was feeling as proud as a peacock tonight showing off his new bride when all the while she was only living up to her end of the bargain.

So she'd made love with him today, so what? Don't go reading things into lovemaking, he warned himself. How many times had he been on the other end of that scenario? How many times did he pretend to feel something that just wasn't there?

Reid felt a tightening in his chest. God, but it hurt to think that Rachel felt that way about him. That he was just a means to an end for her, a father, a protector, a provider for their child.

But what more should he expect from her? Hell, he hardly knew her, and vice versa. Why should she have feelings for him when people who were supposed to love him couldn't find any reason to do so?

Grow up, Reid, and get real. You've gotten what you asked for—she's here, she married you, and the baby will be a part of your life.

Don't push it.

Don't ask for any more.

Like always... you'll be disappointed.

Nine

With the first snowfall in late November, Jules's words became prophetic. Reid's lawn had long stopped requiring his attention. He began traveling into New York to his office once a week. By Christmas, it was two days a week, and after the new year began, he was gone Monday, Wednesday and Friday.

The baby was growing bigger by the day, and Rachel forced herself to wear what she considered ugly but infinitely more comfortable maternity dresses or slacks and smocks. Her monthly doctor's visit produced a sonagram that showed a healthy, growing baby but no determination on the sex, which suited both her and Reid just fine.

In February Rachel busied herself with fixing up the baby's room, giving in to a nesting instinct that she would have scoffed at only months before. She got to know many of the shopkeepers in town, and was beginning to feel as if she belonged in this sleepy rural community. She looked married, acted married, and if it weren't for the fact that her husband slept in a room down the stairs from her own, she would have even felt married.

Reid said it was because he didn't want to disturb her. He'd had a computer installed with a hookup to his office so that he could be in touch at all times. Sometimes, he claimed, he worked well into the night. When she protested that she wouldn't be the least bothered, he countered with the logic that she needed her rest, and he would do anything and everything to see that this pregnancy continued on the positive note it had begun.

It made her feel like a fat hen sitting on her eggs, clucking and flapping her wings to get the rooster's attention as he strutted to and fro in the barnyard. She didn't like this confinement, didn't like this pampering. She felt fine, better than fine. She'd been watching her weight, eating fruits and vegetables and exercising. In fact, other than her protruding stomach, she'd never felt more fit in her entire life.

To make matter worse, they didn't make love anymore. Rachel tried to tell herself it was because he was being considerate, but she knew that wasn't true. He'd been sitting right next to her in the doctor's office when her doctor had made it perfectly clear that sexual activity could continue right up to the birth of the baby as long as it was comfortable for her.

Maybe he just wasn't turned on anymore. But that, too, was a lie. She caught him looking at her from time to time; she recognized that look in his eye. And when she'd walked in on him after he'd stepped out of the shower, his instant arousal told her that, belly and all, Reid wasn't as immune to her as he pretended.

It was as if he were emotionally withdrawing from her in anticipation of the baby's birth, and the why of it haunted her. She cursed the fact that she'd set a year's time limit to this experiment, but whenever she tried to approach him on the subject, he always found a way to soothe her fears for the moment before resuming his aloof behavior.

He had said he'd wanted to "live," but if this was his idea of living, she wanted no part of it. She couldn't imagine how bad things would become between them once the baby was born. It was as if he were fighting her, himself, and the love they had begun to feel for each other.

She knew he felt it. His eyes told her so. His hands when he touched her, even in passing, told her so. Every little glance, every little action said so in a hundred ways. But the words were not forthcoming, and Rachel felt as if she were playing "Beat the Clock" as the days and weeks of January gave way to February.

But the time for the baby's birth was fast approaching, and she still hadn't pierced that steel armor he'd erected around his heart. She still didn't know what made him tick. Once she'd brought up the subject of the orphanage and his years growing up, but he made light of it, as if he hadn't had it so bad after all. His answer reminded her of someone who'd had a horrible accident and attempted to bring humor to the retelling of the incident as a means of defense.

She wished there was a way to get through to him, to get beyond his distrust, his hurt, to make him see that she could be more to him—that they could be more to each other—than parents to their child.

The opportunity came like a brilliant flash of light one Sunday morning as they sat facing each other by the fire reading the *Times*. And it came from the best possible source, the one that had brought them together in the first place.

The baby kicked.

Rachel placed her hand over the spot and rubbed. "Reid . . ."

He looked up from the paper. "What is it?"

"Come here." She beckoned.

He stood and walked around the coffee table and leaned over her. "Something wrong?"

Rachel shook her head and swiveled the lounge chair toward him. "No." She took his hand and placed it palm down on the spot where the baby had moved. "Feel."

As if the child knew the difference in touch, a vigorous poke of a hand or a leg hit him squarely in the center of his palm.

"Holy—"

Rachel smiled broadly.

"Does it do that all the time?"

She nodded. "A lot. You're never here when it happens."

Reid took the mild rebuke to his recent absences. He felt he deserved it. But she couldn't know why he was gone so much, she couldn't know it wasn't his interest in the business that was keeping him away.

It was his feelings for her.

The baby was due, and the time for her to make her decision to stay or go would follow soon after. Things had cooled between them after the party, and that had been mostly his doing. Yet at times he felt as if her decision might go in his favor...but he couldn't be sure. He was pulling away, he knew it, but the more he tried, the less he seemed able to stop himself.

It was a lifelong syndrome that he'd thought he might be able to break with Rachel, but apparently, such was not the case. The pattern was established. The minute he found himself connecting to someone, the doubts would begin. Years of therapy hadn't been able to rid him of his inability to commit himself totally, his inability to give all he had to another human being, his inability to trust...to love.

He'd come so close with her. For a time he'd thought, This is it, this is what it feels like. But then the niggling voice would begin to grow louder in his head, making him think twice, making him ignore his emotions, making him rationalize.

Protect yourself, it said. *She won't stay...she'll leave... Just like all the rest.*

In many ways, he knew he was being ridiculous—go or stay, Rachel would still be a part of his life because of the child. But that, he knew now, would not be enough for him. He had never been one to think he could "have it all," had never even entertained the thought, but once Rachel entered his life, the idea took root, had substance, and now it had grown into a gnawing ache inside of him that wouldn't go away.

He no longer just "wanted it all," he wanted a guarantee that he would *have* it all—*all of her,* completely, unconditionally, belonging to him, body and soul—even though he couldn't offer her the same gift of himself.

But that fantasy wasn't in the cards for him, and self-psychoanalysis aside, he'd learned early on how to remove himself bit by bit from a potentially serious situation until he no longer felt anything anymore, until it no longer mattered.

That was exactly what he was doing now. He was releasing himself from her, a piece at a time, in anticipation of the baby's birth...and her moving on.

A feeling of hopelessness washed over him, together with an anger at his own inability to conquer this...deficiency...in himself. He gritted his teeth as a poignant pang of longing gripped his chest. It felt as if a strong fist were squeezing his heart. He knelt down in front of Rachel to stop himself from doubling over.

"Here," Rachel said as she took his hand, pressing it against the spot where the baby kicked. "Do this." She moved her hand in a circular motion. "Sometimes that makes it happen."

Reid obliged, rubbing her belly with the tips of his fingers for a long minute. He almost jumped back when his machinations were rewarded by a sharp poke, followed immediately by an almost wavelike movement across her stomach.

"She's turning." Rachel lowered her voice as if she were in church.

"She?" His voice dropped to a whisper as well.

"Uh-huh."

"How do you know?"

"I don't. I just feel it. Would it bother you?"

"Not at all."

Reid placed his other hand on the moving mound, marveling at the workings of life while at the same time fighting the knot of emotion that had lodged in his throat threatening to cut off his air. His child, part of him, was moving beneath his hand, and all he could think about was himself, his wants, his needs, his insecurities.

He glanced up at Rachel. Her face was radiant, beaming with the light of life that filled her. His emotions were running too high for him to speak. He felt like a raw open wound laying himself at her feet, asking for anything she deemed able to give him.

And all he could see was love...

Didn't she know what she was doing to him? Wasn't it bad enough that he had to see her every day, that she made sure she was up with him at the crack of dawn to say goodbye on the days when he went into the city? Didn't she have any idea that the sight of her drove him wild with want and need, with longing and fear...

He swallowed and laid his head against her belly, away from her eyes, which gave him too much. "This is incredible," he said, his voice a harsh whisper.

"Yes."

The baby stopped moving, and Reid lifted his head. Rachel brought her fingers to his face. Traces of tears filled the crinkles at the corners of his eyes. Rachel felt her heart expand in her chest at the sight. She touched him with her fingertips, gently wiping the wetness away, then brushed the ever-present strands of hair that fell across his forehead.

"Reid..." she whispered, for no one reason, for a hundred.

The sound of his name on her lips floated over him like a gentle summer breeze. Reid raised himself up, leaning his weight against the arms of the lounge chair, his face only inches from hers.

Rachel remained still as his emerald eyes scanned her face. Her heart was filled with hope and beating so loudly, she was sure he could hear it.

Please...please, she silently begged. *Kiss me...do it...I need you so much...*

As if he did, indeed, hear her, Reid slanted his head and kissed her. A mere brushing of his lips against hers, but like the strike of a match, long-held desire flamed between them. A moan escaped his tight throat, and he ignored that nagging little voice and threw caution to the wind.

He began to eat at her lips, to the right, to the left until she opened her mouth wider for him to take her with his tongue the way he longed to take her with his body.

She moved into the kiss, welcoming the expected heat of him, that intense searing of her senses she fantasized about at night when she lay alone in her bed upstairs. She touched her tongue to his, savoring his special taste, so hot and wet and Reid, a taste like nothing else in her world.

Reid shut his eyes tightly, knowing he was losing himself in her, knowing that in another minute he'd take her here on the chair, on the floor, anywhere she'd let him. He should pull away, save himself, have one less memory to plague him when she was gone. He cupped her head in his hands, threading his fingers through her glorious hair, and deepened the kiss, thrusting his tongue into her mouth one last time.

Just one more minute . . . second . . . and then I'll stop it.

But he couldn't stop it. As he pulled away from her lips, his mouth fed on her neck as his hands roamed down her body, cupping her very full breasts so tenderly and reverently, he was surprised when she thrust herself forward into his hands for more. He obliged her, moistening the fabric of her cotton robe with his mouth as he suckled one round nipple, then the other on his way down her body.

The gaping robe fell open, and Rachel watched as Reid pushed it aside. He trailed the backs of his knuckles around the baby mound of her belly to the mound that lay below. Rachel's eyelids fluttered shut in the delight his feather-soft touch elicited. She had never known a hunger this great, not even on their wedding night when she had been sure she would explode if he didn't touch her.

When his fingers finally brushed against her nest of curls, she felt the evidence of her desire seep through her panties. She bit her lip, mortified that he would know how little it took to bring her to the brink. He continued his assault, and her breath quickened. Embarrassed, yes, but not enough to stop him, not enough to push him away, not enough to sit up and retie her robe, not enough to say no to him.

She was wet, so wet, that Reid's hand curled into a fist to stop himself from dipping into her. His body was aroused and straining against his jeans. He unsnapped them and let the zipper pull open on its own from the natural strain.

But that was all he did. He wanted her, but couldn't—wouldn't—take her. Not now when he was ready to burst, when just touching the tip of himself into her might make him lose all rational source of control and thrust forward. He wouldn't hurt her, hurt the baby no matter how raging his desire was.

He looked up at Rachel's face. She licked her bottom lip, the tiny pink end of her tongue peeking out from between her lips. He felt himself swell even more. She wanted him. No, not just want . . . need. Heaven help him, but he loved it that she was as racked by desire as he was, that she needed him as much as he needed her. To be needed was so new to him . . .

There was something he could do for her, for her only and not himself, something selfless, something done without any expectation from her to reciprocate, something that would fulfill her needs without hurting her in any way.

Deliberately, he positioned himself between her legs. The coffee table at his back, he lifted first one leg then the other onto the edge of the table, effectively trapping himself between the two. Then he looked into her expectant eyes, took hold of her hips, and pulled her toward him until she was wide open and vulnerable to him.

Rachel tried to lift herself.

Reid stilled her with a hand on the inside of her thigh. "Let me."

"Reid, I—"

"Rachel . . . please . . ."

It was the "please" that did it. He never pleaded, never begged, and rarely asked her for anything. She didn't know his reasons, but she knew they were important enough to him to use that word. Slowly, Rachel sank back against the cushions.

"Close your eyes," he said softly, "and relax." He kissed the inside of one thigh, then the other. "I want you to enjoy this," he continued as he insinuated a finger into the elastic leg band of her panties. "I want you to just concentrate on *feeling*. Can you do that?"

Reid pushed aside the material of her panties, and Rachel felt the cool air against her woman's flesh. She swallowed hard. "Yes."

"Good." Reid touched her intimately with the tip of his finger, and immediately she blossomed for him. "Oh, sweetheart, you are so perfect, so very, very perfect..."

And then the tip of his tongue replaced the tip of his finger. Rachel's back arched. "Easy..." he whispered, his hot breath fanning her already sensitive skin.

He touched her again with his tongue, more of it this time, licking at her once, twice, three times, until she had to grip the chair to stop herself from calling out to him.

Reid was going as crazy as she. Her scent engulfed him, her taste permeated his senses. And his own body went into overdrive, the zipper of his jeans splitting completely open, separating as if it had a will of its own. He kissed her even more intimately than before, opening his mouth wider, toying with her, playing with her, dipping his tongue into her.

Little whimpers escaped her lips as Rachel writhed beneath the assault of his mouth. She was gone, lost, and so hopelessly in love and one with him that her body began to undulate in unison to the movements of his tongue. Her heart pounding in her chest, she let him take her on a ride through territory so familiar yet at the same time so frighteningly new because of the depth of her feelings for him.

When he slipped his finger into her, the spasms began with such force she cried out the name of every deity known to man, and some she'd made up, ending with a long, moanful, hoarse plea for him to stop the pleasure that was so intense it bordered on pain.

Reid obeyed immediately, his hands shaking as he released her. He sat up on the edge of the coffee table and gently righted her garments. "You are so beautiful," he said, caressing her cheek with his fingertips. "I want you so much."

Rachel reached for him. "We can—"

"We can't."

"But the doctor said—"

"*I* can't."

Reid pushed away from her and stood, breaking all physical contact with her.

Rachel pulled her robe around her and sat up straight in the chair. "Why? Tell me, why?"

"Because it wouldn't be wise."

Rachel shut her eyes for a long moment. She wouldn't beg, wouldn't make a fool out of herself. If he didn't want to make love *with* her, only *to* her, she couldn't force him, could she?

"What wouldn't be wise? Making love with me?" He turned away from her. "This isn't about sex at all, is it, Reid?"

"I thought I made you happy. I thought that was what you wanted."

"Servicing me doesn't make me happy, Reid. Making love has to be mutual. Give and take. It has to *mean* something."

"It means pleasure. I gave you that."

"No, it means love." She took a deep breath. "I love you, Reid."

He looked stunned. "Don't say that."

"Why not?"

"Because it isn't true."

"It is true. Why can't you trust me to know what I feel? You asked me to trust you, and I did. I married you, moved here with you. Why can't you trust me in return?"

Reid didn't answer, just shook his head, negating her words, negating his response, whatever it might have been.

"You have no idea what I'm talking about, do you?" she asked. "And I guess I don't understand you, either," she said.

"I don't expect you to."

She pinned him with her eyes. "Then explain it to me."

He turned away from that look, the one that pleaded with him to be something he could never be, to give things that he could never give. "I can't. It's something...in me. I can't give you what you're looking for."

"Are you saying you can't love anyone? I don't care what happened to you as a child. I don't believe that, Reid."

Reid's eyes narrowed. He couldn't let her do this to him. He couldn't get into this kind of conversation with her. He refused to talk about those days, that time in his life. He never did, not with anyone, not even his therapist had known all of it. It would be too dangerous for him to delve into areas he had no wish to revisit.

"Believe what you wish. You wanted a year, Rachel. I agreed. It's almost up. We've got the baby to think of now. Let's not start cluttering things up with a lot of empty words and promises."

"My words aren't empty to me," she said softly, aching to wrap her arms around him, to pull him close, to break through that wall he'd built around himself and find the man, the love, she knew existed inside.

"You don't know what you're saying. You're emotional right now."

"And you're not?"

His eyes still wet from the tears he'd shed, Reid backed toward the stairs. "Don't confuse my feelings for the child with anything but what they are. There are some things about me you just can't understand."

"Then help me, Reid. Trust me."

He shook his head once, then again, once again negating her offer. He turned and climbed the stairs.

Rachel heard the door to his bedroom shut. The small room at the head of the staircase had become his refuge...his hiding place. Rachel blew out a long-held breath, suddenly tired, weary of trying to fight him when he was doing such a bang-up job of beating up himself.

She lifted herself from the chair and made her way into the kitchen, her heart heavy in her chest with a profound sadness. She wanted to cry, but couldn't, the tears locked away as if she were saving them for later on...when she knew she would really need them.

Filling the teapot with water from the tap, Rachel picked out a herb tea bag from the canister on the kitchen countertop. She set the pot to boil, staring out the back bay window. Snow covered the spot in the cove where they had made love—really made love—in what seemed to her a lifetime ago.

How could it have all gone so wrong in such a short period of time? The night of the party in the city, he had been so happy, so proud to be married to her. Had her doubts and fears killed whatever promise there might have been to make this marriage into more than just one of convenience for the sake of the baby? She couldn't be sure.

All she knew was that the cold winds of winter had brought a change in Reid. The holidays had been the worst, especially when she'd tried to decorate the house for Christmas. She'd remembered his comment about a tree by the fire, and had done her best to make this little house into the home he'd never had.

Instead of cheering him, though, her efforts only seemed to make him more remote. The chill in the house that week had been worse inside than out. She'd seen the cold, green-eyed side of Reid that had greeted her on her meeting with him in his office, the Reid James who showed no outward emotion, only calculated words and logic.

And things had deteriorated ever since. January blended into February with March fast approaching. They lived together as intimate strangers communicating on only the most shallow level about the most basic things.

Rachel folded her arms over her protruding stomach, unconsciously caressing the baby mound as she let her imagination run back to the first time he wanted her, that night when she was a woman to him and not a baby-making machine. Or was she just kidding herself? Was there ever really a time when she was just a woman to him...a woman he wanted... a woman he could love?

She made a mental note to call Trudy tomorrow. If this was the way things were going to go on, she had to make plans. She swallowed hard past the lump in her throat that felt like an orange, not knowing how much longer she could take this, knowing only that she needed to begin thinking about herself, thinking about the baby.

Because like it or not, her time was almost up.

She put her head down, and finally, the tears came.

Reid paced back and forth in his little room. His mind was in a turmoil. He lifted a No. 2 pencil off his desk and began chewing on the end because he was out of toothpicks, and even six months later, he still longed for the solace a cigarette could bring.

His body was hot, hard as a rock, and in gear. And Rachel was still downstairs ripe and ready. What kind of fool was he, anyway, to get hung up with her on a discussion of words? Since when did words mean anything to him at all? How many times had he told a woman he loved her if that was what she wanted to hear? Why was it so hard to do with Rachel?

He stopped in the middle of the room.

Because with Rachel it meant something. With Rachel he was feeling something. With Rachel he was as close to being in love as he had ever been in his life. Maybe he was already in love.

So, go ahead, chum, go on downstairs and tell her. Then take her to bed.

He headed for the door, then stopped himself. No, this wasn't the way to handle it. Making love with her right now would be the worst possible answer to his problem. It would offer only temporary release. The wall would still be there, only with another layer added on top of it. A new memory to savor, remember, torment him in the days ahead.

No, he didn't need sex that badly.

What he had to do was get his mind off it. Reid keyed into his computer, locking on-line with his financial services. As his investment portfolio scrolled the screen, he stopped here and there to review his high-risk accounts. He tapped the down arrow key, and again the words shot out at him: High Risk.

That had pretty much summed him up, didn't it? High risks were the stakes in every game he played, both personal and in business. Then why was he so afraid of one little black-haired, gray-eyed pregnant woman? What was the big deal? What could it matter? He'd get hurt if she walked away. Okay. He'd been hurt before. In spades. So what was the risk? High? Definitely. He looked at the monitor again, the words flashing at him like neon signs on Broadway at midnight. His heart began to pound.

High risk. His whole *life* had been high risk, and it had never frightened him. When was he going to apply those same rules to his love life? To Rachel . . .

He couldn't go on like this, that was for sure. She talked about trust, and she was right. She had trusted him, married him, moved in with him. She'd done whatever he'd asked to make this work, and yet *he* still couldn't trust her enough to tell her the truth about himself.

So what were his choices? *Just do it, man,* he told himself. Lay it all out. On the line. Every bit of it. All the dirty little details of his life. She either understood or she didn't. She either wanted him or she turned away.

Sweat broke out on his brow as the possibilities paraded inside his head. Reid hit the button on the monitor and the screen went black. He turned off the computer, pulled the chewed-up pencil out of his mouth and threw it on the desk.

It's now or never, he thought, pushing out of the swivel chair and heading for the door.

"Did you mean what you said?"

Rachel jumped at the sound of his voice. Heart pounding, she turned to him. "Wh-what did you say?" she asked, wiping at the wetness on her face.

"I asked if you meant what you said. About trying to understand."

She nodded, uncertain where this conversation might lead. "Yes, I mean it."

"Then . . . would you take a ride with me?"

"A ride?"

"Yes. A long one. Do you feel up to it?"

Rachel had no idea what he wanted from her, but she could tell by the intensity of his green stare that it was very, very important that she agree to this. Her instincts told her that something major was in the works if she would just, quite literally, go along for the ride.

"Yes. I'm fine. I'd love to get out for a while."

He nodded. "Okay. I'll warm up the car."

Reid wasn't kidding. It was a very long ride. At times during the trip, Rachel tried to make small talk, but he seemed lost in his thoughts and his answers made little or no sense, so she gave up and turned the radio on. The music soothed her, and once they crossed the George Washington Bridge heading south, Rachel's eyes began to close as the melody lulled her to sleep.

"We're here," he said.

Rachel pushed up in the passenger seat and checked the clock on the dashboard. They'd been driving for more than two hours. She rubbed her face and looked around. They were sitting in the middle of what could only be described as a snow-covered dune. A large, weather-beaten Victorian house with a separate garage filled the space in front of them. It was secluded, nestled behind pines and tall dune grass covered with snow.

Where is here? she wondered, alighting from the car before Reid could make his way around to get her. He took hold of her elbow and guided her up the shoveled walkway to the steps and onto the wraparound porch. The house looked well cared for despite its age. It had what Rachel could only term a clean serenity to it, the quiet punctured only by the sound of rushing winds and nearby surf.

Reid lifted the brass knocker and let it fall once. She looked at him questioningly, but he didn't—or wouldn't—turn his head in her direction. When the door swung open, she began to understand just a little.

This was a convent.

Ten

The woman who opened the door wore a modified black wimple with a starched, white linen border. Her navy blue dress was covered by a gray apron and on her feet were sturdy navy oxfords.

"Reid! What a delightful surprise!" She was obviously a nun of advanced age, but belying her years, she grabbed Reid by the hands and pulled him over the threshold into the large foyer. "Sister Constance! Look who's here," she called out, only to bring an almost-carbon copy of herself swirling into view behind her.

"What is it, Sister Margaret? Oh, my! Reid!"

"Sisters," he said, kissing both on the cheek. "How are you?"

"Fine. Just fine."

Reid recognized the left-unsaid "And you?" asked with only the well-defined, much-practiced, raised-eyebrow-and-slight-motion-of-the-head language that he was sure was de rigueur learning for each and every sister while still a lowly postulant.

"Sister Margaret, Sister Constance... This..." he said quietly, urging Rachel forward, "is my wife, Rachel."

"Your wife!" Both sisters blessed themselves in unison. "Blessed be the Lord."

Reid laughed. "Never thought it would happen, did you?"

Both shook their heads in unison. "No. Never." Then they stepped forward and each nun took one of Rachel's hands. "Welcome, my dear," Sister Margaret said. "You have no idea how much it means for us to meet you."

Sister Constance's gaze centered on Rachel's swollen belly. "Oh, Margaret, look! A baby, too!"

The two sisters' eyes met. They nodded to each other, communicating something only they understood before returning their beneficent gaze to Rachel.

Rachel cleared her throat to regain their attention. "It's a pleasure to meet you, too."

The nuns had no idea, of course, that this was as much a surprise for Rachel as it was for them. She felt a bit uncomfortable standing still under their intense scrutiny with a huge smile plastered on her face. She felt as if she were meeting her in-laws for the first time, and in many ways, she supposed, she was. She felt she should say something, but what, she couldn't imagine. As she contemplated something appropriate, Reid came to her rescue.

"Well, are you two just going to stand there, or are you going to feed me?"

The two sisters dropped Rachel's hands and began to cluck their tongues as they beckoned Rachel forward down the long hall and into what appeared to be an old-fashioned parlor.

"He never changes," Sister Constance said.

"Always had a ravenous appetite, even as a young child," Sister Margaret added as she took Rachel's coat and escorted her to a recliner.

"Now you just make yourselves comfortable, and I'll get some refreshments," Sister Constance said before scurrying toward the kitchen.

Reid didn't sit. Instead, he roamed around the room. Though this wasn't the house he grew up in, the similarities were there. The furniture was the same, and that brought back a slew of memories he usually pushed away on his quick, infrequent visits here. But today was different, today was a day to seep himself in memory, to allow himself to wallow in the good as well as the bad, to show Rachel a side of himself he'd kept hidden for too long.

So he let it happen, fingering the white, silk-crocheted doilies that protected the headrests and armrests of the chairs and sofa, allowing them to remind him of the days when he sat up very straight on that sofa, measuring his height by whether or not his head could reach the doily.

He glanced at Rachel. She was watching him. Her face was serious, her eyes concerned. What did she think of all this? he wondered. Would she be turned off by what she found here today? This had to be so strange to her, sitting here with two old nuns listening to tales of his boyhood. For all her problems with her father, she was used to a traditional family life, and his life had been anything but traditional. Should he tell her all of it? Or dole out the facts in dribs and drabs?

Their eyes met, and he searched for answers, hoping beyond hope that what he was seeing was understanding, love...and not pity. He couldn't take that, not from anyone, ever, but especially not from her.

"It's been a long time," Reid said, "but the place hasn't changed much."

"We're not ones for change now, Reid, you know that," Sister Margaret said, then turned to Rachel to explain. "The house looks the same way it did when Reid brought us here seven years ago. Our convent in Canada burned down, and our dwindling order couldn't afford to rebuild. We were going to be separated, but Reid wouldn't hear of it. He bought this house and moved what was left of us here. He's been very good to us."

"I—I didn't know," Rachel said, and she wondered if this bit of news was the reason for their visit. If he wanted her to see a different, more benevolent side of him, he was certainly succeeding.

Rachel attempted to catch Reid's eye to question him, but he refused to take the bait. He smiled at her, gracing her only with an almost imperceptible shake of the head that told her there was more—much more—to come.

Reid turned to Sister Margaret and gave her a reproachful look. "I'd thought you'd at least have some new furniture."

"I know you sent us money for furniture, but we sent it on to the missions. They need it much more than we do."

Reid shook his head and laughed. "Sister Margaret, you're right. You'll never change."

"Of course not."

Rachel observed the easy banter between Reid and the nun. She felt as if she were in a time warp watching two people from another era. Even the old-fashioned room reeked of tradition and faith. Pictures of saints and small statuettes decorated each table and shelf. Books and tiny votive candles sat on the windowsills. There was no television in the room, and no radio from what she could see. It was a contemplative room, reflecting the quiet nature of its inhabitants.

To think Reid grew up in a place that even resembled this was boggling to the mind.

But it did explain a lot of things. Especially his occasional lapses into an old-fashioned formal way of speaking... not to mention where he'd come up with their need to *consummate* the marriage.

Sister Constance returned with a tea cart and an assorted array of cakes and cookies. She chatted on about Reid as a youth as she poured tea for Reid and Rachel before serving Sister Margaret and herself.

Balancing her cup and saucer, Sister Constance sat on the club chair across from Rachel. "He was a wicked little boy," she said. "Always running in and out of Father Walsh's sacristy, mixing up his vestments. Oh, yes, he was a chore for all of us."

"But he was the most beautiful, sweetest baby you've ever seen," Sister Margaret added. She smiled as she reached over to Reid and placed her hand on top of his.

Rachel sipped her tea and smiled at their reminiscences. "It's amazing he wasn't adopted," she said.

Sister Margaret's hand dropped away and formed a fist on her lap, and the smiles faded.

"Did I say something wrong?" Rachel asked, suddenly aware of the awkward, heavy silence hanging in the room.

Reid's mouth turned into a half grin. "No, Rachel. You didn't. It's a perfectly normal question. In fact, I asked it a lot myself when I was little. Other children were being adopted, but not me." He turned to the sisters with a sad smile. "They told me it was because I was special."

"I don't understand," Rachel said, eager to hear more.

Reid took a deep breath and placed his teacup on the table. "It was really quite simple. Father Walsh was collecting a healthy monthly allowance from my mother's family to care for me. Once I was adopted, the money would stop, and in all likelihood the orphanage would suffer, or perhaps even eventually close down. He made a decision that it was best for all involved if I remained with the orphanage."

Rachel looked at the sisters. "And you knew?" She couldn't help the accusatory tone of her voice.

"Not at first," Sister Margaret said. "But later." She nodded. "Yes, we knew."

"Couldn't you have done anything about it?" Rachel asked.

"No, unfortunately it was in Father Walsh's hands, not ours. You see, my dear, we take vows of poverty, chastity and obedience. We had no choice but to follow Father's instructions."

"So Reid remained at the orphanage," Rachel said.

"Yes, until he was sixteen," Sister Constance said.

"And then?"

Sister Margaret turned to Reid. "You'll have to ask Reid about that."

Rachel's eyes locked with Reid. He laughed openly. "All in good time. I don't want to overload you all at once."

"You won't," Rachel said.

Reid stood and held out his hand to her. "Come on. There's someone else you should meet." He looked to the Sisters. "Is she up to it?"

Sister Margaret turned to Sister Constance. "Is she still asleep?"

Sister Constance nodded. "Yes, I looked in on her while the tea was brewing."

"Then I'll wait," Reid said. "Don't wake her."

"I'm sure she'd want you to," Sister Margaret said. "Why don't you just go up? She'll be thrilled to see you."

"All right," Reid said, and led Rachel toward the staircase in the corner of the room.

"Who am I going to meet?"

"The woman who raised me. Sister Therese. She's quite old now, and suffered a stroke, so she's confined. But it's important you meet her. She's the closest thing I've ever had to a mother."

Rachel took hold of his arm to stop him. "Are you all right with all this?" she asked, gazing into his eyes for any signs of the stress she was sure he must be feeling.

He placed his hand over hers. "I don't think it's ever easy to face your past. Remember how you felt when you returned home to your father's house?" She nodded. "Well, I guess I'm feeling some of that. But actually, I feel surprisingly well," he said, "If I had known it was going to be this easy, I would have done this years ago."

"Come to visit?"

"Told someone."

"No one knows about this place?"

"No one. Except you."

Rachel blinked, taken aback by the gift of trust that she had asked for but never thought he'd be willing to give. She wanted to tell him so, but her throat closed up with emotion, so she did the next best thing. She hugged him, resting her head against his chest as she wrapped her arms around his waist.

"Oh, sweetheart..." he said, lifting his hand to caress her hair. "You make me feel so good."

Rachel lifted her head. "I do?"

"Yeah." He kissed her forehead. "You do."

"I'm glad you brought me here."

He smiled down at her. "Me, too." Extending his hand toward the steps, he asked, "Shall we?"

Rachel nodded and let him lead the way up the winding staircase.

The bedroom was bright, sunlight streaming in through the double windows. It was a simple room with only a twin bed, a small table with a statue and candle, and a photograph... of Reid.

The nun sleeping in the bed was propped up on several pillows. She had a white veil around her head, as if even in sickness, she must observe the dictates of dress for her order. Reid approached her and took hold of her hand, giving it a slight squeeze. Her eyes opened, and slowly, she recognized him.

Sister Therese smiled. "James..."

"Yes," he said. "I'm here." He bent forward and kissed her. "How arc you feeling?"

She nodded her head slowly. "Very happy to see you."

They stared at each other for a long moment, then Reid nudged Rachel next to him. "There's someone I'd like you to meet."

Rachel moved forward into her line of view. "Hello, Sister," she said softly. "It's so nice to meet you."

"This is Rachel, my wife."

"Oh... James... how I've prayed."

Sister Therese raised her hand to motion Rachel closer, and she obliged. She touched her face with a bony finger. "So pretty, James." Her old eyes scanned the length of her. "And a child on the way!" Shc blessed herself with slow deliberation, and shut her eyes in a moment of silent prayer. When she opened them again, she smiled at Rachel. "I can't tell you how happy this makes me. He was a wonderful boy, full of life and love. And then he lost it all. I'm glad he's found it again."

Rachel felt a lump form in her throat as Reid filled Sister Therese in on news of his life. The nun hung on each word he uttered, her face becoming more animated as he spoke. But she tired easily, and Rachel could see, as could Reid, that this visit was taking a toll on her.

"We'd better be going and let you get your rest." He bent to kiss her again. "We'll come back in a few months with the baby."

"I'd like that, James," Sister Therese said, her voice notably weaker than it had been when they'd arrived.

She gave them her blessing, and Rachel could feel the baby move inside her as the nun touched her. They said their goodbyes and left, shutting the door carefully behind them.

Rachel was filled with emotion and questions. "Why does she call you James." Rachel asked as they descended the steps.

Reid gave her a wry grin. "Father Walsh always called me 'the Reid boy'—Reid being my mother's family name. Sister Therese thought it sacrilegious that I didn't have a saint's name, so she called me James."

"And you put the two together?"

"Yes. When I left. At sixteen."

They rounded the corner, returning to the parlor. "What happened when you were sixteen?" she asked.

Reid put his arm around her waist and kissed her on the temple. "I would think you've heard enough for now."

She wrapped her arms around his waist again and rested against him. "No. I'll never tire of learning about you."

Reid dipped his head and kissed her. She opened her mouth for him, longing, need, love, and understanding all mixed up in the offering. He took it, threading his fingers through her hair, holding her head in place as he ravished her mouth.

"You'd better get me out of here," he whispered against her mouth. "I'm feeling decidedly unreligious right now."

Rachel smiled and ran her finger across his bottom lip. "Then we'd better go. We wouldn't want to shock the Sisters."

He kissed her again, this time a short, hard kiss that promised more to come.

"Oh, excuse me!"

They broke apart as Sister Constance swept around the corner and almost bumped into them.

"I was just going to check on Sister Therese."

"She was tiring, so we thought it best to leave," Reid said, never taking his arm from around Rachel.

"Yes, she tires easily now. I'll go up to see if she needs anything."

"Then we'll say our goodbyes, Sister Constance," Reid said. "We need to be on our way."

He hugged the diminutive sister, as did Rachel. "Come back to see us soon," she said.

"We will."

Sister Margaret was waiting to escort them out to the porch. "Take care, both of you," she said as Reid helped Rachel into the car. "And bring the baby to see us!"

Reid and Rachel waved as they pulled out of the driveway.

"Thank you for bringing me here," Rachel said softly once they were on the open road.

"Thank you for not freaking out."

"How could I? They're delightful."

Reid laughed out loud. "That's not a word I would have used for them while I was growing up! They were tough as nails."

"And look at the horrible job they did on you..."

He glanced at her. "I guess I didn't turn out so badly after all."

Rachel scooted over and put her head on his shoulder. "No, not so badly."

They rode in silence for a long time before Rachel asked, "Tell me the rest, Reid."

"The rest isn't as pretty."

"I want to hear it anyway."

This was the hard part. This was the part he didn't want to speak of. This was the part only he knew. But he'd started something by bringing her to see the Sisters. She had a right to know the rest.

Reid didn't answer her right away, as if he had to sort it all out in his own mind first. "I don't know where to start."

"Start at sixteen."

Reid squirmed in his seat, took a deep breath, then blew it out. "When I was sixteen, I found my birth certificate."

"And..."

"And I found out I wasn't illegitimate."

Rachel pushed off his shoulder and turned to look at him. "Tell me."

"I was snooping around Father Walsh's office. I found my file, and my birth certificate was in it. My mother's name was Joan Reid, my father was Xavier Montserrat. She was wealthy English Canadian, he, wealthy French Canadian. I don't need to tell you that the families didn't mesh. They had been married, and the marriage had been annulled."

"Before you were born?"

"Before either one of them even knew I existed. The marriage only lasted five days."

"I don't understand."

"Neither did I. Until I took off from the orphanage and went to look for my mother."

"And you found her."

"Oh, yes. I found her." He paused. "Sometimes I wish to hell I never had. But I did."

"I gather it was not a pleasant experience."

"No, not at all. You see, by then she had remarried, had other children and was the respectable but hopelessly snobbish matron her family had always planned her to be. She didn't want any reminders of her disastrous and scandalous affair from years ago. She told me to go away and never come back."

"How could she? You were her son."

"Not to her. Her parents had forced her to have me, and then they'd arranged for Father Walsh to take me. They were very wealthy and very controlling. She was only fifteen at the time. My father wasn't much older. They had run away and eloped, but neither family wanted the marriage. Both had other plans for their children. It seems after a few days, my mother and father found they didn't really want to be together, either. They were spoiled and selfish, and what they thought was love was only lust. They allowed their parents to annul the marriage."

"What about your father? Why didn't he do something about you?"

"He didn't know about me. Not until I went to see him shortly after the fiasco with my mother. He denied he even fathered a child with her. Told me he'd used protection with my mother, and he could not be my father. There were no tests in those days to prove otherwise, so I had to leave with my tail tucked between my legs."

"That's why you were so leery of me when I came to you..."

"Initially, yes. But it was also the reason I was willing to give you the benefit of the doubt. I'm living proof that condoms don't always work."

"So your mother didn't want you, and your father denied you." She reached out and rubbed his arm. "Oh, Reid, how awful it must have been for you."

"I won't say it was easy. I hated them, and I was angry. Very angry for a very long time. After a few choice words with Father Walsh, I left the orphanage and struck out on my own. I worked my butt off doing every kind of odd job imaginable for years before I landed in that small company upstate. The owner liked me, and when he retired, he gave me a chance to run the place. I bought him out with loans and more guts than brains. But I resold that little place for double the money. That's where it all started. The rest you know."

The rest she knew, but it would take her some time to sort through all that he had told her. The only thing that was very clear to her was that he needed to be loved, and it would take more than just an ordinary love to satisfy him. Reid would need an unconditional love from her because he'd never gotten that from the very people who were supposed to instill that initial trust in him to begin with.

Okay, she could do that. She loved him enough for both of them if that's what it was going to take to get through to him. This wasn't something that was going to happen overnight, she knew that now. His love would have to be nurtured over a lifetime. Rachel touched her stomach, rubbing the baby mound, knowing now that there was no such thing as coincidence. She was meant to meet him that night. They were meant to have this child and to be together.

She was sent to him, and he to her.

Rachel reached over and touched his arm. "Your parents were weak, Reid, and they made a terrible mistake. I'm sure they know that now."

"Perhaps. But that's something I'll never know. All I do know is that, bottom line, they didn't want me."

"Don't say that."

"It's true, Rachel. I came to terms with it a long time ago." He turned to look her in the eye. *"They didn't want me."*

"Stop the car," she said.

Reid looked over at her. "What—"

"Stop the car," she repeated.

Reid obliged her, pulling off to the side of the road and putting the car in park. "What is it?"

She reached up and touched his cheek with her fingertips. "To hell with them. I want you."

She leaned over and kissed him. He kissed her back with an intensity that told her he knew she meant it. When his lips left hers, she looked deeply into his clear green eyes and felt her heart expand in her chest. "*I* want you, Reid James," she repeated. "Very much."

And when they got home that evening, Rachel showed him exactly how much.

Their child was born at dawn on a cloudless spring day in late March. They named her Emily Therese after Rachel's mother and Sister Therese, and it looked as if she was going to have Rachel's dark hair and Reid's green eyes.

Her godfather, Jules, immediately set up a trust fund for her. Charlotte and Trudy, her godmothers, proclaimed her "the most beautiful child in the world." Her parents totally agreed.

They agreed on something else, too.

They agreed they were in love.

Epilogue

He didn't want to be here. He wanted to be home in Connecticut with his wife and daughter, but his meetings had gone late and his wife had urged him not to make the long drive tonight.

Now he was sorry he'd listened.

He switched on the light and climbed the stairs of the town house. He kicked off his shoes and shrugged out of his jacket even before he entered the bedroom.

The room was dark, the air cool as the white curtains billowed out from the night breeze coming through the open window. He pulled off his tie and threw it, unbuttoning and tugging his shirt out of his trousers as he headed toward the white bed.

Where he stopped dead.

She lay on her side, asleep, her hand cradling her head. She wore a white satin nightgown that hugged her body, more rounded and womanly and desirable than before, if that were possible. A smile creased his entire face, and his heart skipped a beat at the so-wanted sight of her.

How could she have known how badly he needed her tonight? Because she just did. Always.

The moon bathed her porcelain skin in pale light as he reached down and touched her cheek with his fingertip. Her eyes opened wide as she awakened, and she smiled at him, reaching up without a word.

Her eyes were like smoke, gray and misty, filled with love and want and desire, and his blood began to rush through his veins with such force that he was sure she could hear it. He sat on the edge of the bed, leaned forward and kissed her. Her lips were warm as he brushed his mouth against hers. He tried to pull back to see her face again, but she would have no part of it. She clasped her hands around his nape and pulled him to her mouth.

She kissed him this time, nibbling at his lips, coaxing them open, touching her tongue to his in dueling love play that set him on fire.

"Make love with me..." she whispered into his mouth.

"Oh, yes, sweetheart....yes..." he answered as he rolled with her to the center of the king-size bed.

He kissed her deeply, sweeping his tongue into her mouth, tasting her with a hunger a lifetime in the making. She met him more than halfway, her passion a worthy match for his own as her hands roamed inside his gaping shirt, scratching at his chest, flicking her nails across his flat male nipples, driving him insane as she rubbed her body back and forth against his.

He glided the straps of her nightgown down and over her full breasts to her waist, flinging it out of his way onto the white carpeting below. Cupping her gently, he blew his warm breath across her sensitive nipples and kissed his way in between the glorious mounds on his way down to her belly.

Her body arched as his mouth reached her dark nest of curls. He tasted her, his tongue growing bolder as she began to melt in his mouth. Her scent was heady, and he shut his eyes to lose himself in her musky heaven.

She moaned and bucked against him, so wet and hot and needy that he knew only one thing would totally satisfy her tonight. And he was more than ready, willing, and able to provide it.

Rising above her, he let her unbuckle his belt and glide the zipper of his pants down. When she reached inside and caressed him, he thought he would lose his mind. But she had other ideas as she stroked the length of him, the width of him, making him hot and hard and as needy as she.

More.

He stared into her eyes for the longest moment before he stripped the rest of the barrier of clothing away. But she was not one to be denied tonight. She pushed him down and straddled him, taking charge, ownership of him, as she slowly positioned her body to accept him, an inch at a time, taking him deep, deeper into her until he was totally and irrevocably hers.

He took pleasure in watching her control each movement, lifting his hips with each thrust, creating a rhythm that was theirs alone, so sweet and pure and full of love that he wondered how he had lived all his life without it.

His emotions were so close to the surface, he knew he was on the brink of letting go. But he wanted to please her as much as just the sight of her pleased him. He ran a thumb up the inside of her thigh, then higher, until he found what he was looking for. Her body jerked as he rubbed that little nub of flesh with a gentle pressure that he knew would bring her over the edge.

And her body didn't disappoint him. She threw herself against him as he felt her tighten around him even more, taking him with her as her spasms of joy carried him along into a place so filled with light that it could only be called . . . love.

She rested her head against his chest, and he entangled his fingers in her hair, knowing that she could hear the beat of his heart, hoping that she knew it beat for her.

He could not remember ever feeling more perfectly at peace as he did now.

A baby's cry alerted them that they were not alone. They smiled at each other, and he rose from the bed, spotting the small bassinet in the corner of the room. He walked over and reached inside, dangling his finger in front of a very hungry little mouth to get her attention.

"Hello, Emily," he said, clucking his tongue at her as she responded to his voice with coos mixed with cries.

He lifted his daughter into his arms and nestled her against his shoulder as he carried her to the bed and placed her at her mother's breast.

He lay beside them, holding them both as the baby nursed, wrapping them in the cocoon of his arms, his protection, and his love.

His wife lifted her head and rested it against his shoulder, their eyes meeting in shared contentment.

"I love you," he whispered, and he bent his head to kiss her face . . . a beautiful face . . . a trusting face . . . a face he loved. . . .

A face in a dream . . . come true.

* * * * *

The movie event of the season has arrived!
On SUNDAY, OCTOBER 29 AND SUNDAY, NOVEMBER 5
you can find romance, excitement and adventure without leaving your house!
Watch for the EXCLUSIVE FIRST SHOWING of two Harlequin movies on the CBS Sunday Afternoon Showcase.
Two BRAND-NEW movies that guarantee heart-stopping adventure, and of course ROMANCE!
Sunday, October 29—At the Midnight Hour
Sunday, November 5—The Awakening
HARLEQUIN®
Silhouette®
CBS95